DESTROYER OF WORLDS

AN ARKANE THRILLER
J.F. PENN

Destroyer of Worlds. An ARKANE Thriller Book 8
Copyright © J.F. Penn (2016). All rights reserved.

www.JFPenn.com

ISBN: 978-1-912105-66-3

Requests to publish work from this book should be sent to:
joanna@CurlUpPress.com

Cover and Interior Design: JD Smith Design

Printed by Lightning Source

www.CurlUpPress.com

"I am become Death, destroyer of worlds."

Bhagavad Gita

CHAPTER 1

London, England. 5.13am

TENDRILS OF CRIMSON DAWN touched the Thames and turned the river to blood as it heralded a new day. The city was quiet, a magical place at this time when millions of people lay still in their beds. The ancient buildings rested before another crazy morning in the maelstrom that was London.

A ray of light caught the face of Big Ben as its hands ticked each second past, marking another cycle in the city. A block away, between Westminster and Soho, pigeons picked at the remnants of last night's revelry in Trafalgar Square, overlooked by the grand facade of the National Gallery. A black cab curved past St Martin-in-the-Fields church, heading towards the Mall and down towards Buckingham Palace. It swooshed through a puddle and muddy water sprayed up onto the pavement as it passed.

The air was chill, the night had not yet left. The square was still in shadow as a squeak of wheels pierced the air. A man in a high-visibility orange jacket pushed his rubbish cart between the fountains under the shadow of Nelson's Column. As he wheeled the cart through the squar~ picked up litter with a slow stoop and glide: san⁀ pings, a lost teddy bear, flyers for the ne. the discarded flotsam of the city. He had se years since immigrating here, but the treasures people threw away still surprised him. Back in India, most of this would be reused and even sold on.

But he would never see his homeland again now.

Sweat beaded on the man's brow, dripping down into the deep lines around his eyes. He whispered a mantra, over and over, as he took those final steps, his lips forming and reforming the sacred words.

Security cameras, ever watchful, tracked his progress across the square. But his cart had a Westminster City Council logo on the side and he wore the uniform of a street cleaner, so he remained unseen. This was the city of many faces and his brown features were nothing special here in London, a place he called home. No matter now though – the gods called for blood and he had been chosen.

He inhaled the cool air and looked up at the bronze lions guarding Nelson's Column, their regal faces composed as they stared back. A skeletal horse stood high above him on the Fourth Plinth of the square, the modern sculpture on this spot changing over time to reflect the shifting city allegiances. A jaunty bow tied around the horse's front leg displayed the electric lights of the stock exchange ticker tape that ran around it. Its sparse rib cage reminded the man of home, the dried bones that washed up on the shore after floods. At least his family would never go hungry again after this.

He wheeled his cart closer to one of the fountains and looked at his watch.

One more minute.

The man bent and put his hands into the water. The coolness on his skin calmed his mind and he splashed some on his face as he whispered a final prayer. He looked up to the sky to see the last stars of night fading into the dawn and smiled. It was still a beautiful world. Perhaps in his next life, he would return to this great city in a different guise.

The man turned back to his cart, lifted the lid of the bin, reached in and pressed a button. There was a moment of stillness, when a shimmer seemed to hang in the air.

Then, the light exploded.

The bomb blast echoed around Westminster, the impact immediately destroying both fountains and blasting a hole in Trafalgar Square. The giant marble column topped with Nelson's statue shattered. The proud bronze lions melted in the blast and the memorial plaques made from enemy cannon tumbled into the crater.

As the echo from the blast died, the shrill sound of sirens broke the air. Alarm bells went off in every building in central London as Buckingham Palace and the Houses of Parliament went into lockdown.

Above the sound of panic, the *chop chop chop* of a helicopter drew closer. It flew from the south, low along the Thames, emerging over the central city like a wraith. It was black with no markings, and those who saw it thought it was a military response to the bomb.

Seconds after the blast, it hovered over Trafalgar Square, directly above the crater. Dust from the blast swirled about it like fog, cloaking it from the cameras. The side doors opened and three men rappelled down thick ropes that snaked into the hole beneath them.

The bomb had laid open hidden levels beneath Trafalgar Square. These levels were not on any official maps, and few were aware of them. They had never been breached.

Until today.

Inside the crater, the men unhooked themselves from their lines, turned head-torches on, and quickly made their way through the smoking rubble to the door of a vault. It was made of thick metal, overlaid with ancient wood and inscribed with occult patterns. It was also criss-crossed with modern steel bars and protected by a high-level electronic security system.

But the lights on the door were flashing orange, blinking from the blast damage.

One of the men attached a magnetic device to the vault control panel. He pressed a key on the pad, his foot tapping as they waited. It wouldn't be long before the scene crawled with military and police. They had to get out of here quickly.

A whirr and a click.

The door opened.

For a moment the men stood at the entrance, their hesitation betraying a moment's doubt about their mission.

Then the leader stepped inside.

He pulled a Geiger counter from his bag and walked into the vault. It stretched into the distance with separate opaque rooms for books, religious artifacts and unknown objects hidden inside, a cornucopia of hidden knowledge.

But they were only here for one thing.

The device beeped and the man turned towards one of the rooms.

"Quickly now!"

The other two men rammed the door with a short metal post, the grating thump echoing through the vault. Once, twice, and then the door crumpled, shuddering on its hinges as they pushed it open.

The leader stepped inside, the light from his head-torch piercing the gloom.

There was a box on a low shelf painted with scenes from the Mahabharata, one of the great Sanskrit epics of ancient India. The man smiled with relief. He picked it up and placed it in his bag.

Together, the men ran from the vault, clipped themselves back onto the lines and were hauled up into the helicopter. They flew off over the city, leaving destruction in their wake.

CHAPTER 2

Mumbai, India. 10.35am

THE MASSIVE STATUE OF the god dominated the room. Its golden surface glinted, reflecting the light of the candles before it as Shiva Nataraja, Lord of the Dance, ushered in the next cycle of destruction and renewal. A wreath of bright orange marigolds, their petals still wet with dew, lay around his neck and the thick smell of them permeated the room, hemmed in by heavy curtains that kept the city out. The calm gaze of the god rested on the dying man in the bed before him. The room was luxurious, a fitting place for the final hours of one of the richest men in Mumbai. But death came for the rich in their towers as well as the poor crouched in the slums down the road, and Vishal Kapoor couldn't buy any more time.

Asha Kapoor stood by the bed, watching her father. She counted his breaths as his chest rose and fell in slow motion. Her fingers lightly stroked the aquamarine silk sari wrapped around her slim body. She had dressed as a good Hindu daughter to please him but his eyes hadn't even opened today.

She walked with soft footsteps to the shrine and looked up at Shiva, his features serene as he gazed into eternity. Mankind was nothing to the divine and yet she had a plan that would cause a ripple in history.

Even the gods would take notice.

The candlelight flickered and she trailed her fingers through the flame, the edge of pain sharpening her senses. Fire represented the end and a new beginning. Her father's body would soon be on the pyre and she would see a new world created after he was gone.

A rattle came from the bed and her father's breath caught in his throat. Asha's fingers tightened until her nails dug into her skin. Could this be the end? Her heart beat faster and a smile played at her lips in anticipation. He had lingered long enough.

The handle rattled on the locked door behind her, then a brisk knock on the wood.

"Asha, are you in there?"

Her brother's voice held a note of concern. Asha took a deep breath. Mahesh had hired the best doctors in Mumbai, but none held out any hope for their father's survival. Vishal had given up on life in the last days, choosing to succumb to his disease. *It's karma*, he had whispered one night as she had read to him from the Mahabharata of the battles of ancient India. His lungs were riddled with cancer caused by chemicals he had inhaled in his years of digging up the earth, first on archaeological digs and later in the mines as he had expanded his business empire.

But Asha was still angry at him for giving in. Despite her ambition to take the business further, her Papa was still the only man she loved. She brushed tears from her cheeks.

Once he was dead, she would take over and make the company greater than he ever had. He would be proud.

She composed her face into that of the concerned daughter. Her long dark hair hung about perfect features, her light coffee skin inherited from her mother, Rani, a Bollywood actress her father had wooed and won. Mahesh had both the looks and the weakness of their mother but Asha had inherited her mind and ambition from her father, and for that she was glad. She opened the door.

"It won't be long now," she whispered, as her brother strode inside the room. "I couldn't bear to have the doctors poking him with needles anymore. He never shied from death and now he will go to the gods peacefully, without all those tubes."

Mahesh reached for her hand and squeezed it.

"You're right. It's how he would want the end to be."

Together they walked to the bedside and looked down on their father. His head faced east according to Hindu custom and, above it, a lamp flickered soft light across his features. Vishal's expression was composed and there was no suffering on it even as he wheezed his final breaths. The Hindu priest had placed a mark of ash on his forehead and his arms lay on top of a simple white sheet. Asha knew that her father would be pleased. Despite his wealth, he preferred the simpler things from the days of his youth.

She leaned down and kissed him on the cheek. His skin was dry and cool against her lips. The prick of tears stung her eyes again but she brushed them away. He would want her to be strong.

Mahesh bent to his father's right ear and whispered a mantra. If his party-boy friends on the Mumbai circuit could see him now, Asha thought. Suddenly the religious good son. Mahesh's movie-star looks and endless money had made him popular before his marriage and many of his friends had tried their chances with Asha. Of course, there had been dalliances in the dark, but none of those men understood her ambition and she had shunned their marriage proposals, much to her father's chagrin. He had tolerated her choice of independence, wanting her to have a love match as he had. There was one man she respected, one whose company she sought. He awaited her now, but she couldn't go to him empty-handed and she shivered a little at the thought of his displeasure.

Asha walked to the window and pulled back the curtain to let some light in. The wall of glass overlooked Back Bay and the Girgaon Chaupati beach on one side, while the other looked out towards the Arabian Sea. From up here in the Malabar Hills, she could see the ocean and endless horizon. The tower was testament to what her father had achieved, working his way up from a young laborer on archaeological digs to one of the richest men in India. His wealth stretched from the ship-breaking yards of Bangladesh to the mines of Karnataka and West Bengal and into the digital age. This very building contained cutting-edge scientific labs and the hub of their e-commerce division.

As Mahesh whispered his mantra, Asha turned back to the statue of Shiva, the god's golden face promising something even more remarkable than what they had already achieved with the company. There had always been rumors about the discovery that propelled her father from obscurity to extreme wealth. Of course, there would always be those who spoke ill of success, but she had seen a look in her father's eyes that told of a darker truth. When he had fallen sick, she had pored through his old diaries from the time before and discovered what he had given up in exchange for money and power.

But that secret was worth much more than everything they had now, and Asha wanted it back.

A gasp came from the bedside.

She turned quickly and strode to the bed, her sari brushing the floor. Vishal Kapoor opened his eyes and stared at the statue of the god as he breathed his last. Asha saw wonder in her father's gaze as Shiva Nataraja began his dance of death, and he slipped into the beyond.

Mahesh wept, silent tears running down his cheeks as he mourned his father.

Asha took a deep breath and as she stepped back towards

the window, her cell phone vibrated in her pocket. She pulled it out to see the text she had been waiting for.

It is done. The package is on its way.

CHAPTER 3

DR MORGAN SIERRA STOOD on the edge of the bomb crater at the center of Trafalgar Square. The air was still thick with dust and she coughed a little, trying not to inhale too much. She ran her fingers through her dark curls and shook her head as she looked down at the destruction below.

The red alert code had beeped on her phone just after dawn and it had taken her less than two hours to get here from her home in Oxford. In that short time, an enormous tarpaulin had been erected over the scene, protecting what lay beneath from the prying eyes of the media. The military guarded the perimeter of the crime scene and the central city was in lockdown. After all, Buckingham Palace and the government buildings of Westminster were only a block away.

The sound of helicopters buzzed overhead with the incessant desire for more news. The media reported a terrorist attack, but Morgan knew it was more than that.

This was a raid on a place that few knew existed, hidden in plain sight although it wasn't on any official plans. Even the Prime Minister wasn't privy to its secrets. Below Trafalgar Square, wound between the foundations of ancient buildings and the modern Tube lines, lay the labyrinthine global headquarters of ARKANE, the Arcane Religious Knowledge And Numinous Experience Institute. The public-facing side consisted of academic papers on religious artifacts and dry conferences in dusty universities, but in reality, ARKANE was a secret agency investigating supernatural mysteries around the world. There were secrets held here that the world wasn't ready for and the vault below the city protected artifacts that could destroy civilization itself. The secrets ARKANE kept below were more than just a threat to a single nation, they could be used for power on a grander scale.

Now the vault had been breached.

Morgan felt the scar on her side throb, and she rubbed at it through her shirt. It pulsed sometimes when she drew close to the darkness, reminding her of the battle with the demon in the Bone Church of Sedlec. The Devil's Bible was down in the vault. Could that have been what was stolen? What else was down there? Part of her desperately wanted to know, while another part wanted to delay that moment of truth just a little longer.

Her stomach churned at the possibilities. Agents had died to bring items here for safekeeping, to hide them from the world and prevent them being used for evil deeds. She had personally added items to the vault, expecting never to see them again, and she still had nightmares of what she had seen in Houska Castle, unleashed from the Gates of Hell. But it seemed that her short leave for recovery was over. As a specialist in the psychology of extremist religion, and with military experience from the Israeli Defense Force, Morgan knew that she would be back in the field as soon as they could get a lead on the bombing.

"Coffee?"

Morgan turned to see her ARKANE partner, agent Jake Timber, holding two steaming cups.

"I think we're going to need a lot more of this today," he said as he offered her one. Jake gave a rueful smile, the corkscrew scar over his left eye crinkling a little, but his dark eyes remained hard as he surveyed the damage to the iconic square.

Morgan lifted the cup to her lips, taking a sip of the bitter black before sighing deeply.

"I can't believe it," she said, shaking her head. "Who did this? Do we know any details yet?"

"Not much," Jake said. "There's bad news, though. Marietti's in hospital. The Director's tough, but he's unconscious and badly injured. Apparently he was working in the lab nearest the vault."

Jake leaned over the edge of the crater. From their vantage point, they could see the top of the vault and the sliced-open spaces that the ARKANE researchers worked in every day. Construction workers in hard hats scurried around the levels, securing metal pipes, beams and other broken parts of the complex below the surface.

"What was he doing down there?" Morgan asked. The Director's office was above ground in a building to the side of the square, part of the public-facing side of ARKANE. He should have been safe.

"He's been increasingly worried about something," Jake said. "I know he's had migraines for months now. Apparently he's been working late every night in the lab, but we don't know what on. At least no one else was here and he's the only one injured. The bombers did a targeted smash and grab."

"Surely Martin can find out what Marietti has been up to?" Morgan said.

Martin Klein was ARKANE's official librarian and data archivist, nicknamed Spooky because of his ability to find patterns in the chaos of information that streamed into the databases every day.

"Apparently Marietti wiped the logs every night after he finished. He really didn't want people to know what he was doing." Jake pointed down into the hole. "Martin's down there right now trying to fix the defenses. The security system was hacked directly after the bombing and that wasn't meant to be possible. He's also checking the vault's inventory to see what's been taken."

"We should get down there," Morgan said.

Together they walked away from the center of the square and down Duncannon Street to a nondescript doorway next to the Halfway to Heaven pub, an appropriate name for one of the hidden entrances to the ARKANE lower levels.

Security was tight and they had to pass automatic biometric checks as well as human defense protocols before being admitted into the lab-level corridors. This end of the building was undamaged and there were technicians working on decoding artifacts, business as usual despite the bombing. Marietti would be pleased, Morgan thought. He hated anyone to waste time and there was always so much more to do to hold back the dark.

They emerged into the exploded section of the complex and dodged around the scaffolding being erected to reinforce the lower levels. The door of the vault was open and Martin Klein peered into the innards of the electronic keypad. He muttered to himself, shaking his head and tapping away on a tablet as he bobbed up and down on the balls of his feet.

"How can we help, Spooky?" Jake said as they approached.

Martin turned with a start, his concentration broken. His shock of blond hair stood up in clumps, a sure sign that he had been tugging at it as he worked.

"Morgan, Jake. Glad you're here." Martin pushed his thin wire-framed glasses up his nose. "I need to show you something."

His fingers danced over the surface of the tablet computer.

"My office is buried," he said, "but I can still access the databases from here." He pulled up video footage of the vault and played a short clip of the attack. He froze the image as one of the intruders lifted a box from the vault, a military balaclava obscuring his face. "They knew what they were looking for. They went directly to this box and then left quickly."

"What's inside?" Morgan asked.

Martin swiped the screen and quickly brought up an inventory of treasures from the vault. Morgan wanted to read the whole list, the researcher in her desperate to know what else was hidden down here. Before joining ARKANE, she had worked at the University of Oxford, specializing in the unexplained between science and faith, that which fell through the gap of psychology and religion. This vault was one of the reasons she had joined ARKANE in the first place. The knowledge and secrets down here haunted her dreams, yet she had been out in the field on missions since arriving, with no time to lose herself in study.

Martin pulled up an image of a bronze statue, a dancing god surrounded by flames.

"Shiva Nataraja," he said. "One of the primary Hindu gods portrayed as the cosmic dancer who is both destroyer and creator. It's a common enough statue in India." Martin pointed out aspects of the figure. "He dances within the flames of the universe and his left hand holds fire, signifying destruction. His left leg is raised and he stands on a demon of ignorance."

"Lord of the Dance," Morgan whispered, bending closer to look at the image. "It's said that Shiva's long dreadlocks come loose as he dances and they smash the stars into each other, destroying the universe. The snake around his waist is Vasuki, one of the *nagas* or snake gods."

"This attack is a lot of effort for just a statue," Jake said as he gestured at the destruction around them.

"It's not even a whole statue," Martin said. "It's only one piece. The notes indicate that the sculpture was broken into four. The dancing Shiva, the flames that surround him, and then the base in two pieces. The ARKANE vault only contained the fire segment." He tapped on the screen again to reveal the history of the piece. "Marietti lodged it here back in the late 1980s, just after he joined ARKANE from the Vatican. But there are no notes as to its provenance, where it was found or why it was in the vault. As you said, Morgan, these statues are common enough in India. There's no indication as to what is so special about this one."

"Go back to the video," Morgan said. There was a detail about it that bothered her. Martin flicked back to the video and they watched it again. Morgan tapped the screen, freezing it as the men entered the vault. The leader used a device to scan the area.

"That looks like a Geiger counter," Morgan said. "Was the statue radioactive?"

Martin nodded. "A little, but there are plenty of other radioactive artifacts down here so it must have a distinctive signature." Jake raised an eyebrow. "Oh, don't worry. That's why the walls are so thick and we discourage people from spending much time inside. But there's nothing in the records as to why the statue was radioactive. Another mystery."

"We need Marietti," Jake said. "How's he doing?"

Martin tapped the screen again and it shifted to display a hospital room. A figure lay on the bed under white sheets, wires from his body attached to machines and the steady beep of monitors pulsed rhythmically from the screen. Graphs showing Marietti's vital signs popped up under the video feed. Martin shook his head.

"He's still unconscious and has been since the military first on scene found him under the rubble. But the doctors have said they could wake him under extreme necessity."

Morgan looked at Jake and saw indecision in his eyes. She knew that he had a history with Marietti and the Director's injuries were severe. Waking him would be dangerous. But she and Jake had both lain in hospital, injured after their battles with demonic forces and human foes. Marietti knew the risks of their job and he would have ordered the same if the circumstances were reversed. Jake turned to Martin.

"Tell the hospital we're coming," he said.

Martin nodded. But as they turned to go, he called them back.

"Wait. Can you … come inside the vault for a minute?"

Morgan frowned at his words and Jake looked as confused as she did, but they followed him into the vault.

"The cameras are down right now," Martin whispered. "It's safer to talk here, but we must hurry."

"What's going on?" Jake asked.

Martin exhaled sharply, steeling himself. "There's no way a breach like this could happen without someone inside leaking specific details. I've also found evidence that someone was monitoring Marietti's movements."

"They knew he was down here?" Morgan said.

"Yes, definitely," Martin said. "I don't think he was meant to survive."

Jake shook his head. "There have been rumors of a power struggle within ARKANE and some are concerned it's been infiltrated by those who would see darkness triumph. It's hard to believe but …"

"'Better to reign in Hell than serve in Heaven?'" Morgan said, quoting *Paradise Lost*.

"Indeed." Martin tapped at his screen. "If you go after this sculpture, you need to proceed carefully and I think we should keep it off-books as much as possible. I'll sort out funds and logistics from here, but keep a low profile if you can."

An hour later, Morgan and Jake walked into the private wing of an exclusive London hospital. Despite the luxury, the smell of antiseptic made Morgan's skin crawl. She and Jake had both spent enough time in hospital after ARKANE missions, albeit not quite as plush as this. Hospitals were not her favorite place.

After clearing security, they found the Director's room. It had a large picture window with reinforced glass looking out over London, stylish furniture and artwork on the walls. But the view didn't matter to this patient. Marietti lay on his back, his eyes closed, his skin sallow. His chest moved up and down as he breathed and the machines around him beeped softly, the rhythm a welcome sign of stability.

Morgan walked to the bed and stood looking down upon him. The Director had lied to her at the beginning of her time with ARKANE, but she had grown to trust him anyway. There were things that he knew, things that would make even the strongest turn away, and yet he had made it his life's work to protect the world's secrets and keep them all safe. But what had he been doing down in the labs last night – and what was the significance of the statue? Why had it been stolen now, after it had been in the vault for years?

It was clear that they knew little about the Director. Even Jake, who had known him the longest, recruited back when he had been in the military in Africa, still knew little of the Director's past. Morgan laid her hand on Marietti's unmoving arm and willed him to wake up. They needed to know what to do next, and usually it was the Director who sent them on a mission. He was stalwart and strong and his shoulders were broad enough to carry all of them.

But now he was reduced to this.

We are so fragile, Morgan thought. *This human frame that seems so strong is easily broken*. Now Marietti was brought low, there was only a thin line between the people of London and the supernatural that crouched in the shadows waiting for darkness to fall so they could claim dominion.

There was a sudden long beep and a line spiked on one of the machines.

Marietti coughed, his body wracked with shudders. Jake pressed the emergency call button by the bedside as Morgan leaned forward and put her hand on the Director's forehead, trying to calm him.

"It's OK," she said, stroking his brow as he shook under her hand. "We're here. You're going to be OK."

Marietti's eyes flew open.

"Don't let the pieces of the statue come together," he whispered, his voice hoarse and cracked. "The weapon is–"

His words were cut off by a gurgle as blood spewed from his mouth. He clutched at Morgan's arm and his fingers tightened around her as a doctor and attendant nurses rushed into the room. Then his body stiffened and he seized, collapsing in convulsions on the bed.

CHAPTER 4

ASHA HEARD THE BEATING blades of the helicopter on its approach to the towers and walked to the window to watch as it hovered and then landed on the helipad. From London, the box had been taken to a private jet and flown immediately back to Mumbai, and then brought here from the airport in the fastest time possible. She smiled to think of what had arrived with it. In the midst of the mourning rituals, she was still playing the compliant sister and devoted daughter. Mahesh wouldn't know what she planned until it was too late.

Minutes later, there was a knock at her office door.

"Come in," she said, turning to face the entrance. She wore a white trouser suit today, the Hindu color of mourning. The curves flattered her lithe figure, and she found that being underestimated as a mere desirable woman helped her.

The door opened and the scarred man, one of her favorite bodyguards, stood in the doorway with a bag in his hand. Asha wanted to run across the room and grab it from him, so desperate was she for what was inside. But such eagerness did not become her position.

"Put it on the desk," she said abruptly, her voice giving no sense of her anticipation.

The man walked across the carpeted floor, his boots leaving dirty marks on the plush rug. His face was staunch but she felt his eyes flick over her.

He placed the bag on her desk and pulled the top flap open so she could see the box inside. Her fingers itched to touch it, to finally hold the sacred statue that her father had prohibited her from searching for. She remembered his cautionary words even now. *It's too dangerous, Asha. We're not ready for the power it can command.*

But she had searched in secret for the last year, tracing her father's history. In his younger years, he had worked on archaeological digs around the world. He had not been religious back then, choosing to call himself Christian or Muslim, Hindu or Buddhist depending on what dig he worked on. He had once been part of a Vatican team excavating in the caves of Ellora. They had found something there, an object of great power.

Now, finally, it was within her grasp.

Asha walked to the desk, her breathing shallow. She rested her hands on top of the bag and looked up at the man.

"Did you look inside?" Her voice was honey soft and smooth. She smiled and let the tip of her tongue touch her lips, wetting them slightly. The man's pupils dilated and he shifted uncomfortably in place. He shook his head, dragging his eyes away from her mouth.

"Of course not, your orders were clear."

She nodded. "Good. Then you may stay and watch."

As Asha pulled the box from the bag, her fingers shook with anticipation. The energy vibrating from it made her heart race. It was painted with bright colors, displaying images of the god Shiva in his various incarnations. In one he was seated cross-legged on a tiger skin, his body painted blue with a snake around his neck. His right hand was raised in blessing and his dreadlocks flowed down to create the River Ganges. The box itself was a priceless work of art, but it wasn't what she sought.

She took a deep breath and lifted the lid.

Her eyes widened. She slammed the lid back down again,

the sharp sound echoing in the room. Her eyes blazed and narrowed as she looked at the man.

"There's only one piece in here. Where's the rest?" Her voice was ice cold, sharp as a dagger.

Fear flickered across the man's face, confusion in his eyes.

"I swear it. This was the only box in the vault with that radioactive signature. We didn't look in it, we didn't take anything. I promise."

Asha pressed the call button on her desk. The door opened and two bodyguards entered the room, their meaty hands resting on their guns as their huge bodies blocked the exit.

"No, please," the man cried. "I'll find the other pieces."

He fell to his knees, his hands reaching towards her in supplication.

Asha ignored him. "Take him to the Kali temple."

The two bodyguards grabbed the man by the arms and dragged him out, still screaming his protest.

As his cries faded, she opened the box again and looked down at the single piece of the statue, the semi-circle of fire that was meant to surround the god. The bronze edges had been filed into flames that would burn the world to dust and herald a new age. She could see how it would fit into the base, but she needed the other pieces to complete the weapon. She had pored through the diaries and journals and there had been nothing about this. Her father and the man he had found it with must have broken it apart and hidden the pieces separately. It was too late to discover the truth from her father, but perhaps the team he had discovered it with were still alive. She would find them and they would speak when faced with the chamber of the goddess.

But first, she had to face her own reckoning.

Asha clenched her fists and pounded on the table in frustration. She was so close.

In the corner of her office was a private lift. She walked

to it with heavy footsteps and pressed the button. She didn't want to face him now, but she had to.

The lift took only seconds to get to the roof garden and Asha walked out into the verdant space beyond. The smell of tropical flowers and the patter of a waterfall filled the air. Up here it was possible to forget that the slums of Mumbai jostled below, crammed full of those millions who eked out a living on the edge of abundance. It was said of India that you could throw away a mango stone and a tree would grow, and up here, that was true. Vishal had planted the garden many years ago when he had first made his fortune and now Asha tended it in his memory.

Palm trees overhead created dappled shade on a stone path made from rocks gathered from all corners of the Kapoor empire. Pebbles from the beaches in Bangladesh where ships were broken up and sold. Glass from the south of Kerala and even precious stones from the forts of Rajasthan.

Huge glass panels high above could be opened and shut electronically, regulating the atmosphere and heat levels. Solar energy gathered from the roof was used throughout the building. The garden was a fusion of modern technology and the inherent natural power of the gods harnessed together, a fitting metaphor for what Asha intended.

But the statue was the key, and she had failed to get it.

She walked on.

A space had been cleared in the corner of the verdant garden in recent months. As her father lay dying, his position weakened, Asha had taken control of the area, making the changes necessary so her guru would come here. She took tentative steps towards the place now.

She stepped out of the greenery into a bare sandy area strewn with sharp stones and ash from cremation grounds. The smell of flowers dissipated, replaced by the stink of human waste and the tang of blood. The trees had been cleared so he sat under direct sunlight, cross-legged, eyes closed, fingers resting on his knees in the *chin mudra* position, thumb and forefinger touching.

He was naked except for a tiny loincloth, his matted dreadlocks hung to his waist, his bushy beard untrimmed. His dark skin was covered in ash dotted with beads of sweat. In front of him was a human skull fashioned into a *kapala* bowl, its interior stained with red and black from blood and rotten flesh.

Asha slipped off her shoes on the edge of the sand and walked barefoot towards him, each step soft and silent even as the sharp stones pricked her feet. Pain and blood only brought her closer to the goddess. She barely breathed and her heart pounded, as it always did when she approached him. She sank to her knees with no regard for her fine clothes. They meant nothing here. She was no longer a desirable woman, heiress to one of the biggest companies in India. Here she was just an acolyte in front of her guru. She rested her hands upon her knees and bowed her head.

"You do not have it."

His voice was rough and guttural and it grated across her skin. There was disappointment in his tone and Asha felt his judgement like the stripe of the whip. She shivered a little even under the hot sun. This man had a direct line to the gods. He was a sadhu, a holy man, an Aghori, considered the most extreme of their kind and renounced by other sects for their use of the dead in ritual.

The Aghori believed that by transcending social taboo, they could pierce the illusion of reality. If Shiva was perfect and created everything, even those things considered disgusting and rotten must also be perfect and therefore brought the devotee closer to God. Being near the dead allowed the living to understand what really mattered.

Asha had met the Aghori a year ago, when she had attended a Hindu pilgrimage with her father. But they had brought a luxurious tent, fine linen and ample food with them. As Asha had watched the beggars calling out to the gods, she realized that they were closer to the divine than she could ever be in her rich lifestyle.

She had found him while wandering the pilgrim's camp one day, wearing only a simple cotton sari, no makeup, her hair loose about her face, disguised as a woman of simple means. His rejection of material things drew her to him and his devotion to the goddess Kali made her his disciple. Her father had hated the Aghori and while he was alive, her guru was banned, but now she kept him close.

"I have one piece," she said softly. "And I will find the others."

He opened his eyes, the dark pupils ringed with ash, flakes of blood dusting his eyelashes. Asha felt convicted in his gaze.

"You must hurry," he whispered. "The ritual must be performed on the most auspicious day, when the sacrifice will be the greatest, and the power of the weapon will demonstrate the might of Shiva."

"I will have the pieces in time." Asha's voice was strong and she met his gaze with an unblinking stare. "The statue will be whole. I promise."

The Aghori reached for the *kapala* skull and turned it over. He pulled out a sharp knife, then held his hand out and sliced his palm. He drew the blade slowly across his flesh so the blood welled and dripped into the skull.

Asha could hardly breathe as he clenched his palm and let the drops fall. The sight of blood excited her, reminded her of what awaited in the temple of Kali.

But that would have to wait.

The Aghori dipped his finger in the blood and then leaned forward. He pressed it against Asha's forehead, marking her with the crimson liquid. She smelled the coppery tang over the sweat of his body and she closed her eyes as he touched her. He was the only one who anchored her to what was real, and through him she would see God.

CHAPTER 5

"He's coding! Get the crash cart!"

As the high-pitched whine of the machines sounded the alarm, Morgan and Jake stepped back to let the medical team do their work. The doctor injected something into the line in Marietti's arm and a moment later, his body relaxed. He sank back on the bed, still once again.

The doctor turned.

"He's in a bad way so I've sedated him." He shook his head. "His body just needs time to rest and heal."

"How much time?" Jake asked.

The doctor frowned. "It's hard to say. His wounds are extensive. The blast shook his brain as well as his body. You'd better go. There's nothing you can do here."

At the door, Jake turned to look back at Marietti, now prone on the bed. His face creased with concern for the Director.

"We have to find out more about that statue," he said. "And why Marietti put that piece in the vault."

"We could go to his house," Morgan suggested. "See if there's anything we can find there about his past. If there's nothing in the databases, I can't see any other way."

Jake nodded. "Good idea. I visited once years back, the only time he ever had a party, apparently. It was an interesting gathering. Politicians, priests, and people whose names were definitely not their real ones. But then, he mostly kept his life private."

"It's our only option," Morgan said. "Marietti said that the pieces shouldn't come together again, and something about a weapon. We can't wait for him to recover."

"Let's go."

Marietti's house was in a quiet street north of Hampstead Heath. It was a simple two-up, two-down in a terrace and didn't look like much from the outside. It wasn't what Morgan would have expected from the Director, but then she hadn't really considered where he lived before. She associated him with his office overlooking Trafalgar Square, where the only personal touch was the fine art he borrowed from the various art galleries of London. Every time she went in there, he had a new one on the wall.

Spring was just beginning to show on the Heath, with the tips of daffodils starting to protrude from the renewed earth, and the white bells of snowdrops peeking out from under the hedgerows. This part of London had an edge of wildness and people came from all over the city for a glimpse of nature. Morgan could see how Marietti would find some kind of peace here, and she imagined him walking across the Heath in his quiet time, looking up at the trees, maybe smiling at the squirrels as they foraged. The Heath teemed with Londoners at the weekend, and perhaps it reminded him of why he worked for ARKANE. Why they all took the risks they did.

Jake took a set of keys from his pocket. They jangled as he searched through for the right one.

"He gave me a key a while back," he said, noting the inquisitive look on Morgan's face. He raised an eyebrow with a cheeky grin. "You can give me one of yours if you like. Just in case."

Morgan elbowed him in the ribs, smiling a little as they pushed inside. The reality was that they all knew so little about each other beyond the ARKANE missions. She and

Jake had come close a number of times to taking things into the more personal realm, but their missions had gotten in the way.

And perhaps that was for the best.

Marietti's house looked like it hadn't been redecorated since the 1970s. The man was clearly more concerned with his work, and he certainly spent most of his waking hours at the ARKANE offices. It smelled musty, as if the windows hadn't been opened in a long time. There was a picture by the door, a young Marietti with a broad smile on his face, standing next to an archaeological dig. Morgan didn't recognize that smile, for the Director was known for being staunch, unsmiling, serious in the face of almost constant threat.

"So what exactly are we actually looking for?" Jake asked as they walked inside.

"Martin said that Marietti put the sculpture in the vaults in the 1980s," Morgan replied, walking softly down the hall. Every step felt like a trespass, even though she knew the Director would want them to pursue every lead. "We should look for something about his history back then. He said he didn't want the pieces to be put back together again, but where *are* the other pieces?"

Jake frowned. "Because whoever wanted the piece in the vault must surely want the others."

"Exactly," Morgan said. "So we need to get to them first."

They entered the main living area, evidently the room of a bachelor. A wingback chair sat near the window with a view out over the Heath. There was another chair near the door, but the place was not set up for conversation. A pile of books lay near the leather chair and Morgan crouched down to look at them. The history of nuclear war. The physics of nuclear weapons. An introduction to Hindu mythology.

"How do these relate to each other?" Morgan opened the book on nuclear weapons. "I would expect Hindu mythology, but why this interest in nuclear tech? It doesn't seem like something ARKANE would usually be involved in."

ARKANE investigated mysteries of the supernatural, those outside the auspices of other agencies and the police. They were called in when things weren't quite normal, when the explanation for an event couldn't be found in the rational world.

"Marietti was involved in so many things." Jake poked his head into the kitchen, adjoining the living room. "I don't think there was a limit to his curiosity, so this could have just been personal interest."

"But apart from the saber rattling over Iran and North Korea, the world is much safer in terms of the nuclear threat these days," Morgan said.

She picked up another book, a pop-science paperback on particle physics. She leafed through it, the words pretty much meaningless since her own speciality was psychology and religion and the impact of war on both. This leafy suburb of Hampstead was so far from the war zone of Israel, where she had grown up and begun her studies, but she felt the echoes of conflict here. The book had a few color images in the middle and she flicked through the pages to them. One immediately caught her eye.

"Jake, look at this." She held out the page. It showed a massive sculpture of Shiva Nataraja outside the headquarters of CERN, the largest particle physics laboratory in the world, based outside Geneva in Switzerland.

"What is a Shiva statue representing the end of the world doing at a nuclear research lab?" Morgan said. "We need to check that out."

Jake nodded. "It's a start, but I think there's more to be found here."

He circled back to a shelf near the kitchen containing an eclectic range of books as well as a number of photo albums. They were old, from the time when photos were more precious, when film was expensive and people would take a roll and only one of the photos would be worth printing. Jake pulled an album down and leafed through it.

Morgan came to stand at his shoulder. She was so close that she could smell his aftershave and feel the warmth coming from his body. She was glad they were working together again. In their last mission together, he had been critically injured and she had finished the Gates of Hell mission alone. Then he'd gone to New York. He hadn't told her much of what had occurred there but he had certainly returned a stronger man, with no indication of the injuries he had sustained only a few months ago. Just another secret they kept from each other.

The photos in the album showed Marietti as a priest, standing stiffly in front of various famous world monuments. They were trophy photos, markers of his travels but nothing that could help them in particular. Jake picked up another album and flicked through. Then he stopped on a page.

"That certainly brings back memories," he said softly.

The photo showed a group of soldiers, both black and white, standing before a mud hut in a clearing. Marietti stood on the end of the line and Morgan could just make out the Vatican cross sewn on his uniform. Next to him was a younger Jake.

"When was that?" Morgan couldn't help but reach out to touch the photo. Jake's face had fewer lines and there was no corkscrew scar above his eye. But there was still a sense of the wild animal in the way he stood, a young lion holding his power in check, desperate for the hunt. These days, he was still lithe and muscular but he had learned to use that power more effectively.

"Early '90s," Jake said. "I met Marietti in the Sudan. The war was brutal but we were told not to intervene. Marietti was sent as a representative from the Vatican because the Islamic Front was slaughtering Catholics. He understood powerlessness at a time when I still believed that we could solve every problem the world had. I probably would have died fighting there without his counsel."

"Was he ever your friend?" Morgan whispered.

"It was never a two-way relationship, to be honest. He was more like my father back then but since he was made Director, we haven't shared so much personally." Jake turned to Morgan, his eyes bright. She could see his determination. "He will recover, I know he will. He's a fighter. And if he wants to stop the pieces of the statue being brought together again, we'll do that for him."

Morgan nodded. "Then we need to track down those pieces before whoever blew the vault finds them. We should look at the photos from the 1980s, before you met him."

Jake pulled all the albums from the shelf and together they searched through, trying to order them by year. There were no labels on the photos, no text describing the images. Either Marietti had a perfect memory of all these people in all these places, or he was trying to protect his past even as he held onto these tokens of what had once been. Morgan reckoned it was probably the latter.

A page fell open to show Marietti standing with a group at the edge of a mass grave, the outline of individual bodies blurred by the sheer number of them. Jake's face darkened.

"Rwanda," he said, his eyes clouding over. "Those were dark times."

"Why would he keep a picture like that?" Morgan asked.

"It's the most recent genocide in living memory," Jake whispered. "A testament to man's ability to destroy himself. Marietti believed that we all have within us the ability to create or destroy, and that battle can be individual or borne out at this tribal level. He told me once that it was a lesson he wished to remember always."

He turned the page to happier times.

"The Taj Mahal," Jake said, holding out the album to

Morgan. "That smile suggests he knew the person taking the photo well. We need to find out what he was doing in India back then."

Jake took out his smart phone and took some pictures of the images. Then he closed the album gently and placed everything back on the shelf as they had found it.

"It's strange being in here without an invitation," he said.

"I know how you feel," Morgan replied. "But none of us share our personal space with each other right now. I've never even been to your place."

Jake stepped closer, his face only inches from hers. The chemistry between them had been building for so long now, and Morgan wanted to lean into him.

"Are you angling for an invitation?" he said softly.

Morgan's phone rang, the shrill tone breaking the moment between them.

CHAPTER 6

ASHA CHANGED INTO A simple yellow sari and cleaned off her expensive makeup. By adopting the posture and attitude of a lower-class woman and taking off the trappings of wealth, she could roam the streets of Mumbai without notice. Just another solitary figure in a city of millions trying to scrape a living.

Her father forbade such excursions into the city streets alone, but she had been doing it since she was a teenager, determined to learn about the city she lived in and not just from the side of the rich. Over the years, she had developed her own network and her own projects.

She emerged from the basement of Kapoor Towers to a blast of hot air from the street outside. The sound of tooting horns, ringing bells and vendors hawking their goods welcomed her into the bustling city. Mumbai was on a peninsula and so the city had stretched far north and across the bay as it grew. But here, in the oldest part, the only way to grow was to build up.

Asha adjusted her headscarf, pulling it over her face to obscure her fine features from anyone who looked too closely, and walked a few streets before hailing a taxi.

"Dharavi," she said. "Sion-Mahim entrance."

Soon, they pulled in next to the Dharavi slum, founded in 1882 during the British era and home to nearly a million people. Many workers ended up here when they arrived in the city from the rural areas seeking work, and like the rest of Mumbai, Dharavi was full of enterprising entrepreneurs. Pottery, textiles and tanning works crammed into the space along with other production sites and a growing waste and recycling enterprise.

The urban poor in Mumbai worked hard and Asha always found the people here to be an inspiration. She preferred their grafting attitude to that of the entitled young people she had grown up with, obsessed only with fashion and practicing the latest Bollywood dance instead of working. And while she could hold her own at the pinnacle of the Mumbai socialite scene, she actually preferred to walk the streets here in the slum.

She splashed through a puddle, lifting the hem of her sari to avoid getting it wet. The dank water smelled of chemicals used in the tanning process and the air reeked of rubbish and sewers, overlaid with the constant smell of cooking.

Asha weaved her way through the streets, head down in the manner of a good wife hurrying home to her family. She liked to walk unseen, and she had perfected the look of a downtrodden lower-caste woman since she had first started coming here years ago.

She turned a sharp corner and entered the health clinic. She was known here only as the go-between for a rich benefactor who provided funds for the clinic and the shelter for unwanted children and young mothers fallen upon hard times.

"Ms Shah." The receptionist looked surprised as she walked in. "We weren't expecting you today. I'll let the doctor know you're here."

Asha nodded. "Tell her to take her time. I'll be in the day room."

She walked through into a large open area where groups of young women sat, some with babies on their laps, others obviously pregnant. The sound of chatter filled the room as they wove baskets and gossiped as they worked.

The clinic was open to all religions and although the slum was mostly Hindu, it also had a large Muslim population. The girls here were often victims of abuse who had run from home fearing retribution in a culture that still blamed women for sexual attack.

Asha understood the feeling of being marginalized, but these women were part of her bigger plan – even if they weren't aware of it. Every woman and child had blood samples taken when they asked for help, and anything interesting was sent to her lab for testing. The slum was a melting pot and as Asha looked around the room, she saw myriad genetic codes in their faces. She smiled at the thought.

"I'm sorry. I didn't know you were coming." The doctor looked worried as she approached, a brown paper bag clutched in her hand. "I'm about to start surgery."

"I just came to see whether you needed anything."

The doctor looked at her more closely. "And presumably for the latest batch."

Sometimes Asha considered removing the woman, silencing her unspoken questions. But the doctor worked for a pittance and helped more girls here than seemed possible with the number of hours in one day. Asha admired her. In her softer moments, she wondered if she could have been this doctor in another life.

But she was meant for bigger things. The goddess had far more in store for her.

"Come," the doctor said, looking around at the room full of young mothers. "We can't talk in here."

They walked into an adjoining examination room and the doctor pushed the door shut. She handed Asha the bag. There was a jar inside filled with an opaque liquid and something meaty that touched the sides with its bulk.

"Miscarriage," the doctor said. "A child of incest, as you requested."

There was a hint of disgust in her voice, perhaps at her own betrayal of those she served.

Asha pulled a thick wad of rupees from her bag and gave it to the doctor. "There's more when you need it. Make sure you notify me of any new specimens like this."

The doctor folded the money into the pocket of her coat and walked out, slamming the door behind her. Asha didn't mind the doctor's moral concern. The tissue would be used for a greater good.

She headed back to Kapoor Towers, the specimen jar hidden in her bag.

With her Masters degree in Biochemistry, she had taken her interest in genetics even further in the last few years and, with company funding, she had expanded the lab, driven by her own history. Her mother had died of a rare tropical disease that she had caught on one of Vishal's business trips. She'd had some kind of genetic inability to recover from it and had been dead within a day of getting sick. That discovery had fueled Asha's own passion for genetics, in the hope that somehow she could go back in time and save her mother, or at least those who suffered in the same way.

Even as Mahesh had taken responsibility for the mining side of the company, Asha had developed Kapoor Labs, focusing on gene editing. There were several floors dedicated to science, and she oversaw most of them, with each department reporting in weekly on progress. But she had a side project going, something at the intersection of faith and science. She grabbed her white coat and tied back her hair into a neat bun as she entered the lab area.

She pushed open the glass door to the inner labs, where a small team reported directly to her. Nico had his back to her as she entered, bent over a microscope to look at the finer detail of a slide. The door whooshed closed behind her and he turned at the sound.

"I wasn't expecting you until later, Miss Kapoor," he said. "I haven't quite finished the assessment of the latest round."

"I have a new sample with possible mutation to add to

the mix," Asha said. She put the paper bag in one of the medical fridges.

"I'll get to it next," Nico said.

He was tall, his dark hair cut close to his skull. His lanky frame was evidence that he cared more for the experiments in the lab than he did for his own health. He had studied molecular biology and genetic engineering at Harvard, before a stint in China working on CRISPR technology, altering the genetic makeup of crops. He had been part of the team that worked on the first editing of human genomes, although he had avoided the ethical debate that sprang up after the release of their findings.

Asha had found him then and offered him so much money that he had agreed to come back to India for her special project. This lab was not listed as part of the official company assets and much of what they did here was off-books. But along with her search for the weapon, this was Asha's passion.

"Another new specimen arrived today," Nico said. "I haven't even opened the box yet, but it's marked for the Naga project."

He gestured at a polystyrene specimen box sitting on the lab benchtop, marked as bio-hazardous genetic material. Asha grinned.

"I love presents."

She walked over and grabbed a scalpel. She cut the string and pulled open the top of the box. A small snake lay inside, some kind of cobra by the look of it. It had three heads and a lump where a fourth had been growing, but it was a juvenile and couldn't have lived very long.

"That's fantastic," Asha said. She looked at the label and checked the laboratory that sent it. "Is this from the same group that sent the fetus with the extra arm buds?"

Nico nodded. "They're doing good work. Not sure where they're getting the specimens from, though."

Asha held up a hand. "It doesn't matter, as long as they send them to us."

She had long desired to create a living version of one of the many-armed deities of Hindu mythology. Nico had wanted to try Ganesha because of his popularity and the fact that he only had four arms, although he also had an elephant head. But Asha doubted that they would be able to graft such an animal onto a human body as well as grow the extra arms.

Her own fixation was the goddess Kali, one of the aspects of Durga. Depicted with four arms, Kali would be an eminently more practical choice for a hybrid. They were also progressing well with the *naga*, the seven-headed king cobra. The snake represented eternity, eating its own tail in the *ouroboros*, creation into destruction, an echo of the Shiva Nataraja.

While Mahesh focused on earthly power and the wealth they could dig up from the ground, Asha understood the power of inspiration and how the people would follow miracles and wonders. The faithful would rise up at the signs she would bring forth and this would bring even more to pilgrimage on that great day. The more who came to worship, the greater the sacrifice and the more powerful the weapon. It didn't matter that these signs and wonders were built in the lab rather than occurring naturally.

India was on the forefront of technology in the finest scientific tradition, but it was also still mired in myth and daily ritual. Asha wanted to fire a revival of devotion to Kali, for the people to flock back to the gods. That would make the sacrifice so much sweeter.

"Show me where we are on the Kali project," she asked.

Nico walked to the back of the lab and entered a code on a panel. A door slid open.

It was dark inside and as they entered the lights flickered on, revealing a row of tanks. Each one held a specimen, a human fetus at various stages of growth, all attached to tubes, simulating artificial wombs. Some had two arms and extra buds where other limbs had begun to grow. Others had multiple fully-formed limbs and one even had two heads.

Asha smiled at what they had achieved and walked over to one of the tanks to gaze down at their creation. Nico came to stand next to her.

"You know they will never breathe," he whispered. "They will never grow up into the mature deities that people could actually worship."

"It doesn't matter," Asha said. "A dead child with the aspect of a goddess will still inspire millions to pilgrimage. We're so close now."

CHAPTER 7

MARIETTI COULDN'T OPEN HIS eyes but he knew where he was by the antiseptic smell, a vain attempt to banish the stench of the sick and the dying. There was a heaviness in his limbs and the pain of his injuries throbbed in time with his heartbeat even as the sedatives kept him in a semi-aware state.

Dark shadows hovered around the edge of his consciousness and he sensed the beating of black leathery wings about him. There were many who would relish his end, but Marietti was not ready to give up yet. Not with so much at stake.

A sound outside the door drew his attention.

But it was only the voices of the nursing staff as they passed, chattering about the latest episode of some TV program.

He was safe, for now at least, and Marietti found himself slipping into the past, back when he was still a priest – to the time before they had even found the statue, .

Vatican City, Rome. March 16, 1981

Elias Marietti stepped out of his tiny flat in the back streets of Vatican City. He walked to the corner shop for his daily espresso and knocked it back with enthusiasm, a welcome wakeup jolt of energy to start the day.

The sounds of the city wound about him as he walked along the street: the distinctive exhaust from a Vespa motorbike, the shout from an angry driver trying to navigate the crowded streets, the call of a street vendor selling fresh vegetables brought in from the countryside this morning. Marietti loved Rome – not just the sense of power and history that lay under the streets, but also for how close real life was here. The Church was the beating heart of Rome, whereas in other places, it was only peripheral. When he was here he understood his purpose and his place in the world, but the further he traveled from it, the more the ties loosened and doubts crept in.

Now his step was jaunty and a smile played about his lips as he walked. Today could be momentous because late last night, he had found a hint of something buried in the archives, something that had been covered up as part of a larger purpose. It might be the key to what he sought.

Marietti worked within the Vatican Secret Archives, or the Archivum Secretum Apostolicum Vaticanum in the proper Latin. It officially contained the historical records of great world events spanning twelve centuries. Of course, there were famous documents held there that all knew about: Pope Leo X's 1521 decree excommunicating Martin Luther that sparked the Protestant Reformation; the 1493 papal bull that split the New World between Spain and Portugal after Columbus landed in North America. Even the transcripts of Vatican trials against the Knights Templar and later, Galileo.

That official part of the archives had been opened up to scholars in 1881 and were hardly secret. No doubt there were still treasures to be found in the eighty-five kilometers of shelving and over 35,000 volumes, but those public documents were not what excited Marietti today. He worked in the part that still remained behind closed doors in a section that few knew about, let alone were allowed access to.

He smoked a Nazionali cigarette as he walked, enjoying

the warm sun on his face and the smoky taste in his mouth. He could just about live without women and possessions as his vows dictated, but he would struggle to give up his twin addictions of cigarettes and coffee. Thankfully, Vatican City ran on both substances so it was unlikely that he would ever have to choose. He reflected on the document that he had found last night as he walked through the streets towards the Archives. Officially, no materials dated after 1939 were available to scholars because the Vatican still protected Pope Pius XII's involvement with the Nazis in the Second World War. There were many who did not want the truth of that time to be made known. But Marietti was part of a task force dedicated to delving into the occult layer beneath that history.

He had led an expedition to Antarctica in 1979 in the expectation of finding a treasure trove of artifacts, but instead they had only found more papers. These had been taken back to the Vatican and they were still going through the millions of pages. At least his German had improved and he had become adept at understanding the doublespeak of the Reich.

It had been hard at first to ignore the casual comments about the Final Solution and racist rhetoric, but he had learned to skim over much of it. That part was not his focus. The Nazis had taken art and treasures from the people they murdered, and Heinrich Himmler in particular had been obsessed with discovering items of ancient power that would help them win against the Allies.

Marietti had been going through a diary of Himmler's last night and he had found a comment that intrigued him. But it had been late, and his eyes had been tired.

Today he would look anew at the document and his heart beat a little faster at what he might find.

Marietti walked along the Via di Porta Angelica through the Porta di Santa Anna to the entrance of the Archives, adjacent to the Vatican Library. He showed his pass to the guard on the gate and the man nodded him through.

The courtyard beyond was busy as scholars arrived for their designated entry times. Swiss Guards in their colorful uniforms manned the security post at the gate from the Cortile del Belvedere. The blue and mustard striped uniform with Renaissance-style puffed sleeves did nothing to disguise the swift professionalism of the Swiss Guard, highly trained soldiers responsible for the security of the Pope and the Holy See.

Marietti showed his credentials again. One of the soldiers took it and looked more closely at him, matching his features to the photo. Despite his daily entry, security was on high alert as there had been threats against Pope John Paul II and every care was being taken to minimize risk.

After a minute, Marietti was waved through. The high ceilinged corridors smelled of an antique store overlaid with lavender furniture polish, as the cleaning of the Vatican never stopped. It echoed with the footsteps of those hurrying to the various parts of the archive and he strode along with them, a grin on his face as he considered what he might find today.

After navigating the twisted corridors, Marietti finally entered the room that his small team were using to examine the Nazi papers. There was a huge wooden desk of dark wood in the middle, surrounded by towering shelves of old books behind glass.

One of the task force's research assistants, Joseph Manfredi, was there already. The younger man leaned over the desk, examining the document that Marietti had left open late last night. Manfredi turned as the door creaked and his cheeks flushed a little under the light down of his blond facial hair.

"You're here early," Joseph stammered. "I didn't expect you so soon. You were still here when I left last night." He pointed at the document on the desk. "Is this what it looks like?"

Marietti pulled on a pair of thin white gloves used to handle fragile documents. He pointed at the document.

"Look at the notes on the edge of the page." There were doodles and scribbled phrases, streams of consciousness documenting the author's train of thought. "These match Himmler's handwriting." Marietti turned the page. "But this is what I'm really interested in."

It was a hand-drawn map of the Indian sub-continent, rough lines representing the world as it was back in the early 1940s. There were marks on the map and a large black swastika drawn with thick lines in the corner. The swastika had been corrupted by the Reich, although it originally came from ancient India and was used by many world civilizations. It represented the principle of creation, the four swirling arms representing the four directions or the four faces of Brahman, God. Hindus drew swastika symbols on doorposts to welcome the goddess Lakshmi to bring good luck and it was associated with the sun, a positive symbol that had been perverted by the Nazis for their dark purposes.

"The Nazis believed in a pure Aryan race," Marietti said. "This ancient tribe supposedly invaded India thousands of years ago and started the hierarchy of castes, where some individuals were worth more than others. As a young man in the SS, Himmler considered the Kshatriya warrior caste as a model for the Nazi forces. He even carried a copy of the Bhagavad Gita and referred to Krishna's instructions that one should satisfy duty on the battlefield. He required his men to have a pure conscience around killing for a higher purpose."

"Of course, I've heard these rumors of Himmler's obsession with India," Joseph said.

"But this is the first time we've found a map, albeit a rough one." Marietti grinned. "This is what we've been looking for."

He pointed at one of Himmler's comments in the margin of the document. "It sounds as if they found the potential location of a fabled treasure, buried in an Indian cave system."

"Could it be one of the books of the Nine Unknown Men?" Joseph's eyes glittered at the possibility. The Nine Unknown had sworn to protect the most dangerous knowledge of ancient India and many sought their hidden books of power.

"Perhaps," Marietti said. "We just have to figure out what these dots represent." He pulled an old atlas from the shelf. As he turned the pages to a map of India, the smell of spices drifted out.

"The largest mark is here, and I think I know where that is."

CHAPTER 8

As she paced the office in front of the glass window, Asha stopped at every turn to look out over the city. She could just about make out the tiffin-wallahs delivering hot lunches to the downtown offices. Time ticked past and she wasn't any closer to getting the other pieces of the sculpture. Everything had to be ready in time and she could not fail the Aghori. But where were the other pieces?

Her father had looked at this view every day, and yet she didn't know his mind well enough to decipher where he might have hidden them. She thought back over her father's life. The key to their hiding place would be to understand what had meant the most to him.

She turned and looked around the office.

There were pictures on the wall: Vishal with the Prime Minister after the last election and with a Bollywood star at a glitzy launch, another of him wearing a hard hat in front of the ship-breaking yard, and still another in front of one of the mine entrances. She stopped for a moment in front of a picture of the three of them, Mahesh on his lap and Asha herself leaning against her father's knee, looking up with a smile. It had been soon after their mother's death, yet he had made sure they were cared for and never felt alone. She touched her father's face through the glass with a gentle fingertip.

He had certainly doted on his children when he had time to spend with them, which hadn't been often, but Asha knew that he had been proud of both her and Mahesh. Despite that pride, she guessed that Vishal had really seen his legacy as the company and the hundreds of thousands of lives he was responsible for. Perhaps that meant the sculpture fragment was somewhere in this building, within the pinnacle of what he had created, as a representative piece of his empire?

But no, she thought.

The flower garden on the rooftop was a better representation of what he truly valued. When Vishal had found out he was dying, all he had wanted was the sun on his face and the refreshment of a simple glass of water in the heat of the day. He had shed all worldly desires. In the evenings, when his pain was at its worst, he would muse on mortality. He even laughed about it, because all his wealth and power could not prevent the end coming when the gods decided it was time.

He died well, Asha thought. She intended to go with such dignity when it was her time and face her goddess with open eyes.

In those last days, Vishal had gone every day to the Towers of Silence, tall circular structures used to expose the dead according to the Zoroastrian religion. The bodies of the dead were left for scavenging birds to consume the flesh and pick the bones until nothing was left. In this way, the unclean body, considered by some to be possessed by the Corpse Demon, could not pollute the sacred earth.

Asha turned to the wall of glass, looking north towards where the Towers of Silence lay not far from here. She narrowed her eyes. Could a piece be there?

She pressed the intercom button on her desk.

"I need a car out front," she said. "And get me the driver who used to take my father in his last months."

After a moment, the receptionist buzzed back.

"The driver will be downstairs in ten minutes," she said.

Her father's preferred driver was an older man and he snapped to attention as Asha walked towards the sedan car. He didn't meet her eyes but stood looking forward, his back ramrod straight. He wore a dark suit with a white shirt and blue tie with the Kapoor ship logo on it. His shoes were perfectly shined. It was as if he had been waiting for the call to drive even though his master had passed on. Her father had always fostered this kind of dedication in people and Asha smiled at the man.

"I need you to take me to where you used to take my father in those last days."

"Yes ma'am." He nodded. "And I'm so sorry for your loss. Your father was a great man."

His dark eyes were full of sorrow and Asha made a mental note to ensure the man was looked after. Her father would have wanted that.

They drove slowly through the streets of Mumbai and Asha stared out at the crowds through the dark tinted window, a centimeter of glass shielding her from the pollution of the roads, muting the noise of horns. Driving in Mumbai was barely worth it, but she relished the time to think on the short trip.

"Mr Kapoor had special permission to visit from the Parsi community," the driver said, after a few minutes. "Only people of faith can enter the holy grounds."

"But you know someone there, don't you?" Asha said, her voice sweet as honey, her smile open and honest. "I just need to know what my father was thinking in those last days." She let the tears well up and one perfect drop slid down her cheek. She brushed it away. "I miss him so much."

The driver looked stricken at her frailty and Asha turned her head so he couldn't see through her artifice. "Of course. I can try, ma'am."

They soon pulled up next to a locked gate with signs on it prohibiting access to the Towers of Silence. A dense tangle of trees and flowers could be seen behind, barely contained by the walls, and behind it, they could just see the top of the tower.

"Please wait here," the driver said. "I'll ring my contact."

"Here," Asha said, handing the driver a wad of rupees. "This may help."

The driver got out of the car and made a call. A few minutes later, a thin man came to the gate and unlocked it. The two men spoke together in hushed tones and money changed hands before the driver beckoned. Asha pulled a headscarf on, covering her face in modesty, and stepped out of the car.

"This man will take you to the tower," the driver said. "He knew your father in those last days."

The thin man led Asha through the garden. The sound of Mumbai retreated as the dense foliage created a fecund barrier to the encroaching city. They emerged from the verdant green at the side of the tower and walked up two flights of stairs to a small platform overlooking the inner chambers.

"Your father would sit here for hours," the thin man said. "I would share my chai with him sometimes if the wind blew up and he began to shiver. But he wouldn't move until his prayers were done." The man shook his head. "Funny really, because he wasn't even Parsi. He didn't really understand our faith, but he certainly understood death. I'll leave you for a time."

From where she stood, Asha couldn't see what lay at the base of the tower. She waited until the man's footsteps faded before she stepped forward to look down.

There were three concentric walls: the bodies of men lay in the outer ring, women in the second, and children in the middle. There were several corpses in various stages of decomposition lying in the pit. A man, little more than a skeleton with tufts of flesh like growths upon his bones. Two tiny bodies of children curled around each other. Asha wondered how they had died and whether they found comfort together in death.

There was an ossuary pit at the center of the tower for the collection of bones once they had been bleached by the sun and scoured by the wind and rain. Lime was added to help the disintegration and the matter filtered through multiple levels of coal and sand until eventually nothing was left.

It was simple and stark and Asha understood why they did this, for what is human life but the world incarnate, made flesh for a time. Then we must all return to dust, our bodies subsiding back into nature. It wasn't shocking. There was no real sense of anything human left here.

The cry of a vulture broke the air and a huge bird flapped down to peck at what remained of the man's corpse. Asha had read that the vultures here were under threat. Their numbers were dropping and there were not enough of the carrion birds to devour the bodies from the Parsi community. Even the ancient rituals of death were under threat in the march to modernity that transformed India day by day.

She gazed down at the bodies and tried to find a way into her father's mind. What had he thought about when he sat here? Had he considered the sculpture? Had he even thought of it at all? She had to believe that he had, and if so, what impact would this place have on where he might have hidden it?

A ray of sun burst through the clouds above and lighted on the innermost ring where the bodies of the children lay. The shadows shifted and Asha suddenly saw the outline of a trapdoor.

There was something underneath.

She ran down the stairs, lifting her sari out of the way so she didn't trip in her haste. Her headscarf fell onto her shoulders, but she was beyond caring about modesty.

"Excuse me," she called. The thin man emerged from a stone arch holding a cup of chai.

"Are you OK, ma'am?"

"There's a trapdoor in the middle of the tower," Asha said. "I need to know what's down there."

"The sacred area of the ritual precinct can only be entered

by the *nusessalars*, the pallbearers," he said. "They look after the bodies and that's their way to the circles of the dead."

"I need to see it." There was a hard edge to Asha's voice. She no longer played the submissive woman. She was Asha Kapoor, one of the richest and most powerful women in India.

The man hesitated. "I'm sorry, but I can't let you in there."

"You let my father in."

The man sighed and nodded slowly.

"But he was dying, and you are not."

"We're all dying," Asha said softly. "The question is when and how much pain we suffer … and whether our families go with us."

The man paled at the clear threat in her voice.

"Come."

He led her through the stone arch and down some stairs. The smell of rotting flesh and the almost sweet stench of decomposition filled the air, but the corridors were swept clean. The bodies were outside, up above, and strangely these underground passages were for the living. Asha had no sense of dread here, only anticipation at what she might find.

Their footsteps echoed in the narrow passageway as they walked towards the center of the tower and the man stopped in a circular antechamber.

"I can go no further," he said. "My faith forbids it. But if you must, then step that way." He pointed at one of the archways from the narrow room.

Asha walked onwards alone.

The passageway opened up into a round chamber where a spiral staircase wound its way up to the trapdoor in the ceiling. There were two stone slabs, evidently for washing bodies before they were taken above. There were niches in the walls where bodies could be laid in waiting but all were empty now.

It was still and quiet and Asha felt at peace. She didn't flinch before death, and this was death's waiting room. She believed the physical body was nothing but a vessel and that the true self would be reincarnated. She wondered what her father would come back as, or if he had escaped the cycle of Samsara. She intended to earn such great karma with her deeds that she would escape the cycle this time around. But for such a sacrifice that would gain the attention of the gods, she needed the complete statue. She walked around the stone chamber, wondering what her father had thought when he was down here.

Then, something caught her eye.

There was a carving on the wall, a tiny ship etched into the stone. She walked closer and bent down. The stone had been recently replaced, the mortar around it crumbled and the edges more polished than adjacent stones. The ship was a crude rendition of the Kapoor company logo, a nod to Vishal's first billion from the ship-breaking industry. Strange to see it in this place. It had to mean something.

Asha pulled a nail file from her bag and used it to chip away at the mortar around the stone. It fell away quickly and she levered the rock from its place. Behind it was a box. As she moved to let the light fall upon it, she gasped aloud, her inhalation echoing around the room.

How could this be?

She reached in with trembling fingers and pulled the box out.

It was made from cedar wood and decorated with dots and swirls from the paintbrush of a child. She hugged it close as she remembered painting it alongside Mahesh when they were young. Vishal had said that it would honor their mother if they painted it with love. He had kept her ashes in it and Asha had thought it safe in the family vault, so why was it here?

The box was heavy – heavier than it should be if it only contained ash, but she resisted opening it. She didn't want to see the physical remains of the mother who had loved her. But her father had clearly come here in his last days, desperate to hide something precious in a place guarded by death.

Asha opened the box.

It was filled with grey dust, like sand from a forgotten beach. There was nothing here of her mother and Asha steeled herself. She poked the ashes with the nail file, swirling it around until she heard a chink of metal against metal.

She levered the file and a corner of bronze emerged from the dust. She pulled it from the box, uncaring now of the grains that clung to her fingertips. It was one half of the base of the Shiva Nataraja statue.

A triumphant glow flushed over her body. The Aghori would be pleased and he would bless her. The day of sacrifice ticked closer, but she still had time to find the other two pieces.

Asha closed the lid, hiding the sculpture again, and laid the box gently in her bag. She replaced the stone and smoothed the mortar back into place, then she ran her fingers over the carving of the ship. Perhaps it was a clue to where her father had hidden the next piece?

CHAPTER 9

THE ENERGY BETWEEN MORGAN and Jake crackled before she stepped away.

"Another time," she whispered. She answered the phone. "What is it, Martin?"

She put the phone on speaker and his tinny voice filled the room.

"I've looked back through the ARKANE database at Marietti's official history. It's patchy and I'm still trying to get more details from the Vatican Secret Archives. He was working closely with them back in the 1980s. But when he was in India he worked with a man called Vishal Kapoor, who became one of India's richest billionaires. There are, as yet unconfirmed, reports that he died yesterday. It's not public knowledge yet because of the potential effect on his company's share price, but we'll confirm it later today."

"He couldn't have ordered the raid, then," Morgan said.

"But the timing is too coincidental," Jake added.

"I'll keep digging," Martin said. "But in the meantime, there's something you should look at right away. Vishal Kapoor was one of the team who donated the statue of Shiva Nataraja to the CERN laboratory in Switzerland. He went with the statue to deliver it and his company was heavily involved in the nuclear program in India." The sound of tapping came from the phone. "I've booked you both on a flight to Geneva. By the time you get there, I should know more about the background between Vishal and Marietti."

* * *

The plane banked over Lake Geneva towards the airport near the border of Switzerland and France. The lake sparkled in the sun and Morgan leaned closer to the window, resting her head on the glass to get a better look. The water below was calm and deep blue and she longed to dive into the depths. It had been too long since she'd had time to lie back and relax in the waves. Growing up with her father in Israel, they had often gone swimming in the Mediterranean. His favorite place on the coast was Caesarea beach where they could swim next to an ancient Roman aqueduct, built by King Herod in the first century. There were never any lifeguards there and she could clamber on the ancient rocks, poking into crevices to see what she could find. Not something that would be allowed here in Switzerland, of course. No clambering on monuments here, ancient or otherwise.

"Do you ski?" Jake asked, breaking her thoughts as he leaned over to look out the window. "It's not too far to Chamonix from here."

"Not very well." Morgan grinned. "But I could probably beat you at surfing a sand dune."

Jake laughed. "I might have to take you up on that sometime." He pulled out his smart phone, opening the notes on the CERN laboratory that Martin had sent through. "So this place is basically trying to explain the universe?"

"They study the nature of matter," Morgan said. "Most people have only heard of the Large Hadron Collider, the huge twenty-seven kilometer ring built underground beneath the border between France and Switzerland. They accelerate particles and then slam them together and see what happens." She tilted her head. "Well, that's the basic explanation anyway."

Jake grinned. "Sounds like a fun place."

"There are a ton of conspiracy theories, of course," Morgan continued. "Some think that the Collider is some kind of alien portal, like a stargate. Or that the particle accelerator could destroy the world with antimatter."

Jake raised an eyebrow, his corkscrew scar crinkling. "You and I have seen enough to know that there is often some truth behind the conspiracy theories."

Morgan nodded. "But I think it's more likely that people just don't understand the physics – I certainly don't. But CERN has been at the cutting edge of scientific discovery since 1954. This is where Tim Berners-Lee invented the World Wide Web back in 1989. Get a load of scientists together and see what they come up with. It's a great idea."

"Maybe we need to do something like that for the supernatural world?" Jake mused. "Imagine how much fun we'd have."

The plane descended for landing and Morgan and Jake soon emerged into the arrivals hall. A young Indian man stood holding a sign with their names on it, his eyes scanning the crowd. They walked over and he greeted them.

"Welcome to Geneva," he said, with a faint Indian accent. "I'll be taking you on your tour today. I'm Amit, a research scientist on secondment here, so I can answer all your questions. This way."

He led them to a black sedan and they got in.

"It's not far," he said. "I'll take you to the visitor center first."

They soon pulled up in front of a huge golfball-shaped structure, the high dome evoking the circular shape of the Large Hadron Collider. Morgan wondered what secrets they kept here, deep under the earth, away from the prying eyes of interested tourists.

"I understand that you want to see the statue of Shiva?" Amit said, as they climbed out of the car and stretched their legs. "I can take you there straightaway. As a Hindu, I'm proud that my country donated the statue to the lab."

They followed Amit down a winding path beyond the visitor center towards more lab buildings, all labelled to help tell them apart. It was a huge campus and Morgan looked around in interest as they walked, wondering what really went on here. Perhaps like ARKANE it had a public-facing side, publishing the findings that were understandable to people in some way. But she was sure that they found things here that were unexplainable, indistinguishable from magic as Arthur C. Clarke said of any sufficiently advanced technology. Once she would have laughed at the idea of conspiracy, but she had seen things with ARKANE that made anything possible.

"What does the statue represent to you as a Hindu and a scientist?" Jake asked.

Amit paused, his face serious.

"Lord Shiva danced the universe into existence. He sustains it and eventually, he will destroy it. Whether you see this as a metaphor or an ancient truth, it's a powerful symbol for what we study here: the very building blocks of the universe. I believe that even if we find the answer to every scientific question, beyond that will still be God, the great unknowable. The American cosmologist Carl Sagan spoke of the parallel between Shiva Nataraja and subatomic physics. He understood the Hindu idea of cycles of time, an infinite number of deaths and rebirths. To understand this is to realize our own insignificant place in the universe." Amit paused and then pointed onwards. "This way."

They rounded a corner between buildings 39 and 40, a short distance from the main building, and suddenly there it was. A two-meter-high copper statue of Shiva Nataraja. Morgan walked closer, drawn to the smooth skin of the god as his almond-shaped eyes stared implacably down at her.

"It was made using an ancient technique of bronze casting," Amit explained. "The original sculpture was made from wax, each perfect detail carved according to the exact image of Shiva, for each statue must be perfect in homage to God. A clay cast was made and then the wax melted from inside before metal was poured into the space left behind. The clay was chipped away, leaving the bronze statue, which was then filed and polished to create the final piece. This is an art that we continue to use in India for many sacred statues."

Jake bent down to read the plaque at the base.

"It's meant to symbolize the marriage of technology and mythology," he said. "Presented by representatives of the Indian Department of Atomic Energy back in 2004."

Morgan walked slowly around the statue, examining it for any other markings. The bronze fire surrounding the god shone in the sun and it seemed as if he could step down from his pedestal at any moment and pound the earth with his heels. She could almost hear the ringing of the hollow bronze and feel the shaking of the ground beneath. The demon under Shiva's feet had an expression of horror as he was crushed, but the god remained calm and expressionless as he renewed creation.

On the back side of the sculpture, behind Shiva's right knee, Morgan noticed scratches in the metal. They were unusual, as the rest of it was so perfectly polished. She bent closer.

"Look at this," she called to Jake. "It looks like a row of numbers, a code of some kind: 2717389178042068."

Amit came closer and as he bent to look at the code, his face paled.

"It can't be," he whispered. "It's just … It must be the artist's mark, some kind of number representing the workshop where it was made." He turned away and Morgan could see that he was shaking. The code was certainly more than an artist's mark. She took a picture with her smart phone and sent it off to Martin Klein back at ARKANE.

"Perhaps you could tell us about the men who donated the statue," Jake said. "We're particularly interested in Vishal Kapoor."

Amit turned, his face still pale from the discovery.

"There's something–"

A gunshot split the air, cutting off his words. A metallic ping echoed from the statue as a bullet hit the bronze.

"Down!" Jake shouted, pulling Amit to the ground.

Morgan crouched low and scooted around the statue away from the direction of the gunfire. They had come unarmed to the research facility, but now she regretted the assumption of a purely academic visit.

She poked her head out quickly and then pulled back as more shots peppered the statue.

"We have to get inside," she said. "They'll be on us soon enough. Before security can get here, at least."

Amit was shaking and his hands clutched at Jake as he whispered desperate prayers.

"The numbers," he said, his voice shaking. "It can't be …"

He stood suddenly and ran towards the main building, stumbling as he pushed himself up. Jake lunged at him, his fingers brushing Amit's coat, but he couldn't get a grasp.

A single shot rang out.

The young scientist fell to the ground, clutching his leg as blood spurted out on the pathway. He screamed in pain.

Alarm bells began to ring and security guards emerged from the building, but Morgan knew that they wouldn't find the shooter. Whoever it was would be long gone, their warning delivered.

As security swarmed towards them. Martin's comments about a leak at ARKANE troubled her. Was this a warning to stop them proceeding any further with the search? Was Marietti in danger?

Jake put his hands on his head and Morgan followed suit. No point in making a scene. They'd be out of here soon enough once Martin got on the case.

"Amit was about to tell us something about Vishal Kapoor," Jake said. "We need to know more about his business and how it relates to nuclear energy."

"And what the hell does that code mean?" Morgan replied. "Hopefully Martin will be able to get something from it so we know where to go next."

Two hours later, after being questioned and searched and ultimately having Martin plead their case remotely to have them set free, Jake and Morgan walked out of CERN and caught a taxi back to the airport. A text came in on Jake's phone and he held it up for Morgan to see.

"It's from Martin," he said. "The code on the statue contained the latitude and longitude references for the Taj Mahal. He's just sorting out flights for Agra."

"I haven't been there for a long time," Morgan whispered, her voice trailing off as she looked out the window at the mountains in the distance.

She closed her eyes for a minute with her head turned away so Jake wouldn't see her expression. She had been to the Taj Mahal on honeymoon with her husband Elian, only months before he had been killed fighting on the Golan Heights. They had both been in the Israeli Defense Force and knew the risks, but their time together had been so brief. Sometimes she could barely summon Elian's face to her mind, let alone recall the touch of his skin on hers.

But the Taj … Morgan sighed softly. She remembered the romance of gazing up at the perfect dome under the full moon as they sailed along the Yamuna River, and later, the opulent hotel in Agra where they had lain entwined for the night. *I will love you forever*, Elian had whispered, *like Shah Jahan loved his queen.* But that great love had ended in tragedy too, and like Shah Jahan, she was the one left behind.

"Martin's arranged a military transport," Jake said, tapping on his phone and interrupting her memories. "We should just be able to make it to the airport in time."

Morgan brushed the hint of tears from her cheek and turned back to Jake. He looked over and grinned, his excitement at the thrill of the chase clear in his expression. Morgan couldn't help but smile back because she knew exactly how he felt. Despite all she had lost, ARKANE gave her more than adventure. It gave her a purpose.

It suddenly struck Morgan that she could summon Jake's face in her sleep now. They had worked together on enough missions and been through so much danger, seen so many unexplainable things. Together, they had experienced far more than she and Elian had ever been through because they had never directly worked together. Her husband had been stationed at the military front while she had worked as a psychologist between Jerusalem and Tel Aviv. Now she spent intense periods with Jake on missions.

There was a spark between them and they both knew it. But the danger they both put themselves in meant the likelihood of loss if they took things any further. Morgan worried so much about her twin sister Faye and her niece Gemma, whom she had endangered at Pentecost. After Elian's death and her father's murder, Morgan didn't think she could handle such a personal loss again.

Of course, she could always give up being an ARKANE agent and return to the University of Oxford as an academic. Life would be simpler and safer, but it would also be black and white. With Jake and ARKANE, she lived in technicolor.

Jake leaned over and showed her some pictures of the Taj on his phone. "It's amazing," he said. "I've always wanted to visit. Do you think one of the pieces could be there?"

"It's possible," Morgan said. "But the Taj attracts millions of visitors every year, and from what I remember, it's not full of obvious places to hide a piece of a statue."

"We'll work it out when we get there," Jake said. "Remember Santiago de Compostela in Spain? We didn't have a clue where the stone was hidden, and yet, we still found it, despite it being hidden for so long."

"You had way too much fun that day," Morgan said with a laugh, as she remembered Jake swinging on the chasuble rope, high up in the nave.

He took her hand in his and squeezed, his dark eyes suddenly serious. "We're a good team, Morgan. I'm glad we're doing this together."

CHAPTER 10

ASHA WALKED INTO THE penthouse office without knocking and breezed past the secretary with a cool glance that stopped the woman in her tracks. Mahesh had begun to use the main office before their father had died but now he had truly made it his own. He looked up as she came in and Asha noticed the dark shadows under his eyes.

"What is it?" he said, his voice tired.

"I hear you're heading to Chittagong," Asha replied.

Mahesh stood and ran his hands through his thick black hair. "Yes, I need to build better relationships with the heads of each industry sector." He looked at his watch. "I'm heading to the airport in an hour."

"I want to come," Asha said. "I've never seen the ship-breaking yards before."

Mahesh looked surprised. "I thought you'd focus on the lab and tech side of things now. I can handle manufacturing and mining. Let's face it, the ship-breaking yard is no place for a woman."

Asha bristled at his words, a retort on the tip of her tongue. But she held it in. She walked to the desk. Mahesh was using their father's fountain pen, a Visconti inlaid with walnut wood. She leaned forward and picked it up, taking the cap off to admire the silver nib.

"He used this for all his legal documents," she said. "His private journals too."

"It's too big for your hand," Mahesh replied, plucking it from her fingers.

She let him take it, forcing herself to relax. She needed to keep him onside for just a little longer.

"We can't split everything between us," Asha said in a softer tone, her voice placating. "Father would have wanted us both to understand all aspects of the business. If you let me come to Chittagong, I'll escort you round the labs when we get back. I have some projects that will fascinate you." She paused for effect and then dropped her head, letting a glimmer of a tear glisten at the corner of her eye. "I miss him."

Mahesh rounded the desk and pulled her close, stroking her long hair. "I miss him too, Ash." He kissed the top of her head. "Let's not fight. I need your support as we go through this transitional period." Asha leaned against her brother and wrapped her arms around him in return. For a moment, she felt her father's warmth in his embrace. Then Mahesh stepped back. "Actually, I could use your help. The Board want me to look into a number of discrepancies. Father's illness put them off but now they want answers."

A chill ran through Asha at his words. The labs, the clinic, the Aghori, the hunt for the pieces of the statue, the Kali temple. All were secret, but there would be a money trail.

"What kind of things are they looking into?" she asked, her eyes wide with innocence.

"The details are all in that report." Mahesh pointed at a thick folder on the desk. "I'm going to skim it on the plane."

Asha's eyes darted to the report. She had to know what was in it. She still needed more time to get the rest of the statue and she could not be found out now.

Mahesh looked at his watch. "If you're coming, I'll meet you on the helipad in ten minutes and we'll head to the airport."

An hour later, they boarded the Kapoor private jet and were soon flying northeast towards Chittagong in Bangladesh, on the Bay of Bengal. It was a six-hour flight across the widest part of India, but at least they traveled in comfort. The stewardess brought refreshments over as Mahesh opened his briefcase and pulled out the Board report.

"How about I skim it and give you the highlights?" Asha said.

Mahesh smiled. "I'm glad to have you here, sis." He handed her the Board report. "Just make sure I can answer all their difficult questions."

They both settled into their respective work as the plane flew east. The hum of the engines soothed Asha as she concentrated on the dense text. Much of it was focused on the main business sectors but as she skimmed through, she found questions raised about funds diverted to her own projects.

Asha visualized the Board, those self-righteous, pompous men who gorged themselves on the profits of others, who had grown fat from the industry of the Kapoors and who now questioned how the company was run. But they had forgotten what lay beneath it all. They had forgotten the man who had scraped and worked his fingers to bloody stumps for his first few dollars. Vishal hadn't been afraid to get his hands dirty in order to build a future for his family, and Asha had every intention of making sure the company continued in that vein.

She worked through the report and by the time the plane descended, she had distilled it into a few pages of summary for Mahesh to read as well as recommended actions for the more innocuous projects. That should keep their attention elsewhere for a little while, Asha thought as she packed up the files and buckled up.

They soon landed in Chittagong, a natural harbor and major coastal seaport city that had seen the Portuguese trade here in the seventeenth century, later the Mughal Empire and then the British East India Company. It had become part of East Pakistan in 1947 after Partition of India, and the city had been the site of Bangladesh's Declaration of Independence in 1971.

Asha knew that her father had an emotional attachment to the ship-breaking yards here. He had been a fixer for various archaeological digs and that had led to him solving problems in many different industries, making relationships across huge cultural and logistical divides. He had become involved in the shipping industry and soon saw an opening for the thorny problem of disposal. Most commercial ships had a lifespan of twenty-five to thirty years, and then became uneconomical due to wear and tear.

Vishal always reused everything, finding ways to recycle even the smallest leftovers. She remembered how he had tinkered with their bikes in the early days of the business, soldering on extra parts he'd sourced from local scrapyards. She could only imagine her father's excitement when faced with a huge ship to break down.

Asha had only seen pictures of the huge rusting hulks in the shallow waters of the coast before. This was the first time she would see them with her own eyes. Could there be another piece of the statue here?

"I know Father would want us to keep the yards running," Mahesh said, as they both stared out the window of the car that drove them north out of the city to the coast. He reached for Asha's hand. "But there have to be changes now he's gone. You understand that, don't you?"

Asha heard the implication in his voice.

"Of course," she said. "Did you have anything specific in mind?"

"Your ... guru." Mahesh spat the word. "If you want to be more involved in the running of the company, you have to get rid of him. We can't be associated with such extremism."

Asha pulled her hand from Mahesh's grasp. Her brother couldn't understand what the Aghori meant to her. She could still feel the touch of his bloody fingers on her skin. She could still hear his sacred words. Mahesh didn't know what they planned, so she just had to play for more time.

"As you wish." Mahesh looked over at her demure words and frowned a little. She looked back with wide eyes. "It's all about what's most important for the company now, I understand that."

Mahesh nodded and was silent for a moment.

"Nalika is pregnant," he said finally. "I meant to tell you, but it's not even three months yet, so we're keeping it quiet."

A dark stone settled in Asha's stomach. A baby would be seen as a success for Mahesh. He would be a responsible family man, a worthy successor to her father. The Board would sideline her. She couldn't let that happen.

She leaned in to give him a hug. "Congratulations," she said, beaming. "I'm so pleased. Did Father know?"

Mahesh shook his head. "I whispered it to him at the end but he didn't respond."

"He would have been pleased," Asha said. "Delighted."

She stared out the window again, focusing on the gulf to the west as they sped north on N1. Another child to add to a nation of over a billion people. What impact could that have on a global scale? None whatsoever. She would prove who was the more powerful sibling.

But time was ticking away.

They finally reached the ship-breaking yards, passed the armed guards and stepped out of the car into the heat of the late afternoon. The tang of burned metal and rust hung in the salty air with a greasy edge of oil that seemed to coat the back of Asha's throat. The dirty beach stretched into the distance with the hulks of old ships in the shallow waters, looming above the sand. Some were fully intact, ready to be picked over, others were just shells, stripped of every useful part. The names of the ships faded in the sun, the paint peeling away as they were returned to the elements.

Thousands of men worked here. They crawled through the beached container ships and oil tankers every day, breaking down everything to its component parts, ants under the gigantic propellers and barnacle-encrusted hulls. It was like the Towers of Silence in a way, Asha thought. That which has been created must be destroyed. Everything was reused here, in the same way that bodies were devoured by the raptor birds in the Parsi towers. She could see why her father had loved it here. It appealed on a visceral scale, an impressive testament to man's power over machine.

The foreman approached, taking his hard hat off as he greeted them. He shook Mahesh's hand and gave Asha a respectful nod.

"I'm so sorry about your father," he said. "He came for an inspection only last year."

"We're here to make sure that everything continues smoothly," Mahesh said.

Asha put her hand on the foreman's arm.

"I want to see what my father did when he was here." Her lips trembled slightly. "I want to trace his footsteps through the yard."

A look of surprise crossed Mahesh's face at her emotional words but he remained silent.

"I'm sorry madam, but that's impossible," the foreman said, trepidation on his face. "Everything changes here by the day, as you can see. The ships come in periodically and every day those that are here disappear little by little. You cannot see what your father saw because it's all gone."

Asha looked out over the vista of metallic grey and noted the pools of rust and oil that slicked about the hulls of the ships. Where could her father have hidden the sculpture piece in these ever-shifting sands?

She nodded. "Of course, I understand, but please show me what you can. I want to see through his eyes."

"This way," the foreman said. "We can stay on the board-walk and keep you out of the mud."

They followed him to the shoreline and onto the rough planks laid down at the edge of the sand.

Men traipsed back and forth through the black mud in

bare feet or simple flip-flops. A group of them walked past with a heavy cable over their shoulders as they dragged it towards a newly arrived ship.

"They'll use that to winch pieces of the ship ashore," the foreman said. "We reuse a lot of the materials and chemicals and we find other special items, too. Your father liked to see those. He had his own special place to do it. Come, I'll show you."

A shrill cry suddenly rang out from one of the ships, taken up by the workers around it. The men shouted as they ran from the shoreline, arms waving in warning. A wrenching squeal of metal tore the air. One side of a nearby ship broke apart and a giant hunk of metal crashed to the sand. The noise was like a muffled explosion and the shock rippled under their feet.

The foreman grabbed Asha's arm, steadying her as the moment passed and the men began to walk back towards the ship again, ready to break the piece down and winch it away. Their nonchalance implied such near-death was a regular event.

They walked on further to a hut on stilts, raised above the mud so it had a view out to the ships unmarred by the proximity of the workers.

"Your father trusted me to choose the most interesting things and leave them in here," the foreman said. "Should I continue this in future?"

"Yes," Mahesh said quickly. "Nothing should change for now."

Asha mounted the steps and pushed open the door.

The room was divided into two, separated by a thick curtain. There was a long table under the window and a simple chair behind it, a red metal toolbox on one side, neatly closed. Asha put out one hand and touched it lightly.

"Remember this?" She turned to Mahesh and he smiled back.

"Of course, he used to get it out even if it was just to change a lightbulb. He was always a fixer. But what was he doing in here?"

Asha flicked open the toolbox, checking in case the statue piece was inside. It was a long shot, but there had to be a reason this place had been so special to Vishal.

Mahesh walked to the back of the room and pulled open the curtain to reveal a rack of shelves, each one jam-packed with items, a cabinet of curiosities from the ships. The shelving included a bunkbed, made up with simple cotton sheets and a wool blanket.

"He must have come here to escape sometimes," Mahesh said. "Perhaps it reminded him of what life was like at the beginning."

Asha smiled. "I can imagine him tinkering away at the table, looking out at the ships." She sat down on the bunk. "Sleeping here." She swung her legs up and curled on top of the blanket.

There was a picture pinned to the bottom of the shelf below. Her father would have looked at it every time he lay here.

The Taj Mahal. The iconic symbol of India.

"Look at this," Asha said, scooting over so her brother could lie down next to her. It felt like they were children again, huddling in a den and hiding from the world. She could feel the warmth of him and for a moment, she wanted to lay her head on his shoulder and forget all the plans she had in place.

"That's where he proposed to Mama." His voice was soft and Asha heard the hint of the little boy who had lost his mother so young. "She was performing there, dancing in a crowd scene for a Bollywood movie. He was still building the business back then so he wasn't rich, but she still said yes."

"He never told me about that," Asha whispered.

"He wanted you to be strong and forge your own path. He didn't want you starry-eyed at the thought of love." Mahesh turned his head to look at the picture again. "He loved the Taj. In fact, he was there when it was designated a UNESCO World Heritage Site in 1983. He advised as to how they could ensure it would stand up to the huge numbers of people who would visit."

Asha looked up at the Taj, resplendent in white marble against the blue skies of Uttar Pradesh. If it had meant so much to her father, perhaps he had hidden another piece of the sculpture there. She would go to Agra next.

CHAPTER 11

MARIETTI LAY ON THE hospital bed, his body prone and unmoving. But there was a flickering under his eyelids, lucid dreaming of a past that now came to haunt him again.

Maharashtra, India. April 19, 1982. 2.43pm

The sun beat down as they trekked along the path towards the caves of Ellora. Sweat dripped down Marietti's back, soaking the shirt he wore under his pack. He pulled the brim of his hat down further to shield his eyes and turned to see how the others were doing.

Joseph Manfredi, his assistant from the Vatican Archives, trudged along several meters behind. His face was beetroot red and he still wore the permanent frown he had adopted since they had landed in Mumbai the day prior. Behind him walked Vishal Kapoor, a trusted local fixer and specialist on Indian archaeology, who had worked on a number of digs for the Vatican.

All three men trailed behind Nataline Reed, a young woman of mixed Indian and British heritage whose brisk walk set the pace. Her specialism was rock-cut architecture and Hindu myth, although she was a devout Catholic from the southern state of Goa. She had long dark hair that curled around soft features and her eyebrows arched in a way that reminded Marietti of the Titian Venus of Urbino. Of course, that painting was of a nude and Marietti kept trying to banish the image from his mind whenever he looked at her. For the first time in his life, he regretted his love of art and how he could bring to mind any painting he had studied over the years. He tried to keep his eyes from Nataline's shapely behind as she strode up the hill, wishing he had time to stop and have a cigarette, or some coffee.

"How much further?" Joseph shouted, unable to keep the tone of annoyance from his voice as he brushed yet another fly from his face. The man was clearly at home in the cool, dry stillness of the Vatican Archives, but out here in the heat and abundance, noise and smells, he was lost. Still, Marietti couldn't do this alone. He needed help and until they found something of significance, this motley crew was all he had.

"Not long, Mr Manfredi, sir," Vishal said with a smile, giving that distinctive Indian head-wobble as he spoke. He was a jolly fellow and Marietti instinctively liked the man, with his willingness to help and the knowledge he so clearly had about Indian archaeology.

They walked around a final corner and Marietti's eyes widened at the huge temple complex. The word 'cave' could not possibly describe the rock-cut edifice in front of him. It reminded him of the glories of the rose-red city of Petra in Jordan or the stone churches of Lalibela in Ethiopia. Nataline stood close by, sipping from her water bottle.

"The Hindu caves here were constructed between the sixth and eighth centuries," she said. "The complex design rivals the great cathedrals of Europe that took generations to build. The architects had such vision." She shook her head in wonder and then pointed up at the stone elephant in front of them. "This is part of the Kailasa temple, designed to resemble Mount Kailash, the dwelling place of Lord Shiva in the Himalaya. It's carved out of a single rock, not constructed from blocks as you would think, and covers an area double the size of the Parthenon in Athens."

"How are we going to find anything here?" Joseph wheezed as he sat heavily on a rock to catch his breath.

"We'll split up," Marietti said. "You and Vishal take the east side."

Joseph looked grateful and headed off into the shade of the temple.

Marietti pulled the page from Himmler's diary out of his backpack. He needed to figure out how the directions of the old map related to the physical layout of the temple. He turned it around and compared it to what lay before him. It just didn't fit. So what was he missing? He tried re-reading the German, a frown deepening between his thick eyebrows.

"I still don't know what you're specifically looking for."

Nataline stood before him. The sun was behind her and he could see the curves of her body silhouetted underneath her loose shirt. He took a deep breath, unable to take his eyes off her as she walked closer, breaking the moment.

"I'm ..." Marietti struggled to recall what he'd been thinking only moments ago. "We're looking for something specific, the Brahmastra. Do you know of it?"

Nataline nodded. "Of course, it's a mythical weapon. Incredibly powerful. Why do you think this place relates to it?"

He opened the diary and explained the background of Himmler's fascination with India and the Nazis' search for the ultimate weapon.

"Do you know of anywhere in the complex that might fit?" he asked.

Nataline gazed out at the setting sun as she thought. After a moment, she spoke.

"There is something. This way."

She led the way through rock corridors to Cave 19 and stopped in front of a carved panel showing a dancing god. The bottom half was plain rock, but higher up where it was harder to reach there were still intricate paintings in yellow, green and white.

"Shiva Nataraja," Nataline said. "The destroyer and creator of the universe. If anything would fascinate the Nazis, it would be this."

Marietti looked more closely at the carved figure as his undulating arms ushered in a new creation. Then he noticed something. The demon of ignorance under Shiva's feet looked out of place, and the stone had weathered in a different way.

"Look at this," he said. Nataline bent close and he could smell a hint of citrus on her skin, a fresh scent that cut through the dense air. Her eyes narrowed.

She bent to her pack and pulled out a makeup kit in a floral bag, the type associated with more high-maintenance women. Marietti smiled as she opened it to reveal a field archaeologist's kit with files, a mini trowel and brushes of various kinds. He was impressed. Even if she had been searched, it's unlikely these would have been discovered.

Nataline brushed gently at the demon.

"There, look. You can see a seam. This was added later. It's not part of the original carving."

"Can you lever it out?"

Nataline raised a perfectly shaped eyebrow. "And damage a world-famous archaeological site?"

"We can put it back after," Marietti said with a grin. "Besides, I know you're itching to find out what's behind it."

Nataline smiled. "Well, if we have the blessing of the Vatican …" She chose a file from her kit and began to pick at the little carving.

"It's protruding quite far out." She gave it a push and it shifted. Her eyes flashed to Marietti's, a look of excitement darting between them. She pushed it again, straining a little. "You do it." She moved sideways to allow him more space.

Marietti used both his hands and pressed the demon forward into the rock. There was an audible thunk and a crunch, the shifting of stone on sand, the rubbing of rocks against each other, and then the whole panel shifted back to reveal an entrance. It was no more than half a meter wide, but enough that they could shuffle through. Inside, all was darkness.

"What is happening, sir?" Vishal appeared from behind a corner of the temple. His eyes widened as he saw the entrance.

"We may have found what we were looking for," Marietti said. "But we need light and tools from the packs we left at the entrance."

"I'll go," Vishal said. "And I'll get Mr Joseph, too. He's resting right now." Vishal's smile said it all, and Marietti knew who he'd rather have next to him in the cave. He nodded.

Vishal dashed off, his feet slip-sliding over the rocks in his haste. Nataline looked at Marietti.

"Do you seriously think that the Brahmastra could be in there?" Her beautiful features twisted in concern.

"It's only a myth," Marietti said. "But there's clearly something worth hiding in this sacred complex. Something the Nazis knew about but were never able to get to."

Vishal soon returned with headlamps and Joseph scrambled behind him.

"What's this I hear about a secret entrance?" he said, enthusiasm returning to his voice at the possibility of finding something. He stopped abruptly as he saw the split rock and the darkness inside. His face fell as Nataline and Marietti donned headlamps. "Oh. We're going in, then?"

"You're welcome to wait out here," Marietti said.

"Can I come, sir?" Vishal said, his eyes bright with excitement.

"Of course." Marietti nodded. "You're the expert, after all."

"I'm coming," Joseph snapped, and they all geared up.

After adjusting their headlamps, Marietti stepped inside the dark passageway first. This was what drove him, the anticipation of what they might find. He knew there were ancient artifacts of power hidden across the world and his mission for the Vatican had always been to find them and bring them back before others could use them for dark deeds. But in recent months, he had wondered what happened to the things he brought back and whether, in fact, they were being used in precisely the way he feared. There were dark times coming and he had heard of a group who stood apart from the church, ARKANE, who collected objects of power and kept them from all religious groups, understanding that they each had their own agenda. When he got back to Rome, he intended to inquire further. It was time for a change.

He felt a crunch under his feet and a crack echoed in the narrow tunnel. Marietti looked down to see the path ahead littered with bones. A thick layer of them stretched into the tunnel, a mixture of small animal and human remains. They disintegrated to dust under his boots.

"Watch your feet," he said as he walked on.

The path wound down through the rock.

"This was clearly part of the original complex," Nataline said as they stepped carefully through the residue of death. She shone her headlamp up the walls. "The paintings are more protected here, and I would guess they date back to the eighth century."

Marietti looked up to see a huge painting of Shiva destroying the world. His long hair whirled out and the stars rained down from heaven in fire that consumed the earth.

"Happy times," he said. What the hell was down here?

They rounded a corner and the tunnel opened up into a huge chamber, so wide that the beam of their lights couldn't reach the other side.

"Hello!" Joseph shouted, his voice echoing round the chamber. Marietti spun and grabbed his arm.

"Hush," he whispered through gritted teeth. "This is a holy place."

"It's not our faith," Joseph snapped, pulling his arm away. "It's all just myth and superstition." He strode into the center of the chamber and spun around. His headlamp darted over rock walls, skipping over paintings of Hindu demons, of the goddess Kali devouring her victims as she clutched their decapitated heads in her many hands. Vishal gasped at the scenes as the light flickered over them.

Then a glint flashed and Joseph stopped, turning back to what they had only glimpsed before.

A statue of Shiva Nataraja in burnished bronze stood upon a stone altar, the intricate figure dancing the world to destruction. There were Sanskrit words inscribed on the base. Joseph strode towards it.

"No." Vishal's voice was thin and reedy in the semi-darkness. "Don't touch it, sir."

Joseph lifted his chin and Marietti saw defiance in his gaze. He had no respect for this land, he only wanted to possess it. Joseph reached out and grabbed the statue, picking it up and holding it above his head.

"What? It's nothing. Just a bronze idol, like the Lord God struck down in Egypt."

Then his face froze in a look of horror. "What was that?" He spun round.

Marietti and the others spun too, but there was nothing there.

"Get away from me!" Joseph's voice was stricken as he stared at the pictures on the walls. He backed away as if the stalking gods came for him. He tried to shake the statue from his hand, but he couldn't prise it away. So he used it as a weapon, whirling around, brandishing it like a club as he beat at the air.

"Get back, you demons of Hell!" he shouted.

Marietti moved towards him.

"The guardians of Shiva are here," Vishal whispered. "He has angered them. Don't touch him."

Joseph began to foam at the mouth, his face growing red in the light. He moaned.

Then he began to scream.

The sound made Marietti's skin crawl and he felt Nataline take his arm.

"We have to help him," she whispered.

Marietti took another step forward, but Vishal held him back.

"The statue is cursed," he said.

Joseph dropped to his knees, wrapping himself around the statue, curving his body over and around it as he whimpered in agony. His headlamp went dark as it hit the ground, but they could see the statue glowing, an unnatural light streaming from it. At last, Joseph's cries died and his body went limp.

Then the light from the statue went out.

Vishal released Marietti's arm. "Go to him now, but don't touch the statue. There are stories of this weapon and harnessing its curse, but it must be treated carefully."

Marietti went to Joseph and together with Nataline they pulled his body from the statue, careful not to touch it.

Joseph's face was frozen in a rictus of horror, his eyes wide and bloodshot as if he had looked into the gaping maw of Hell.

"What did he see?" Nataline murmured as Marietti closed the man's eyes.

"I'd say the demons painted on these walls might have something to do with it." Marietti shuddered. "I wouldn't want to meet any of this lot in the flesh."

"A hallucination perhaps?" she said. "Brought on by touching the statue."

"The ancient civilizations were pretty good with curses and booby traps," Marietti said.

Joseph's skin turned grey as they watched, and then his flesh began to shrivel, wrinkling in on itself. They stepped quickly away as his body crumbled into dust.

"What the–?"

Marietti shook his head. Whatever the statue was, they couldn't leave it here. But could he trust the Vatican with it?

"Mr Marietti, sir. Look at this." Vishal's voice wavered and Marietti turned to see him crouching down by the altar, his head-torch illuminating a mural. It showed a Hindu holy man, standing in Vrksasana, the yogic tree pose, his left leg bent at the knee, his arms above his head. He held the statue of Shiva Nataraja in his hands, his mouth open as he spoke a mantra. Around him, a crowd of thousands drew near. Rays of light streamed from the statue and all it touched shriveled before it, their bodies turning to dust.

Nataline walked closer and bent to read the script around the edge.

"It speaks of the Brahmastra," she said, reaching out with one slim hand to indicate the words. "The statue of Shiva concentrates some kind of power … conjured by speaking a specific holy mantra. Then it feeds off the energy of the dead, amplifying it further. If used incorrectly, it burns those who dare to touch it."

She looked over at the pile of dust on the ground.

"There's more writing here," Vishal said.

Nataline turned to look, her fingers brushing over the ancient words. "The weapon is a messenger of death and can harness the power of a thousand suns for those who know how to use it." Her voice shook. "And it speaks of Harappa."

"An ancient civilization in the Indus Valley," Vishal explained. "They found skeletons scattered along the streets there as if some instantaneous death knocked them down where they stood. The skeletons were still radioactive after thousands of years."

"This weapon is what the Nazis sought," Marietti whispered. "Thank God they never found it."

Nataline looked up, her face pale in the flickering light.

"But there are others who will seek it. We can't leave the statue here now, not this time. If you found out about it, others will too. And look at the Indian government with their nuclear weapons and the ongoing saber rattling with Pakistan. This is too powerful to leave behind."

Vishal gave his customary head wobble. "I agree, sir. This is very bad for my people."

Marietti spun around and paced away from them into the darkness, not wanting them to see his indecision. He looked back at what was left of Joseph's body, the outline of a human corpse barely discernible against the grey rock. He couldn't be sure that the statue would be safe in the Vatican, even in the Secret Archives. There were too many people with contacts in the shadows, those who would barter such an object for temporal power, or use it to spread chaos.

But they couldn't leave it here. Nataline was right, there would be those who would follow in their footsteps.

He turned to look at his two companions, such different people moving in separate worlds, and an idea began to form.

"We could break it apart," he said. "Each take a section and hide it without telling the others where. I'll explain Joseph's … accident to the Vatican and you two can return to your own lives."

Nataline stood, her hands out as if to push him away. She shook her head vehemently. "No, not me. I won't touch that thing." She crossed herself. "I promise to be silent but don't involve me, Elias." She looked up at him and he could see that her eyes were wet with tears.

He walked over and pulled her to him, rubbing her back with his hands. "It's OK," he whispered. "You don't have to do anything you don't want to." He could feel her body under her clothes and he felt a stirring within, a desire to protect and shelter her. She was so fragile. How could he even ask such a thing of her?

"I'll do it," Vishal said. "We can take half each and hide the pieces far away."

Marietti released Nataline and nodded.

Vishal crouched down next to the statue. It lay on its side where it had dropped from Joseph's hands.

"It's stopped glowing. Look, it seems to be only metal again." He used a pocketknife to prod it gingerly.

Nothing happened.

"Let's try with gloves," Marietti said. Vishal looked up with doubt in his eyes. Marietti shrugged. "I'll do it."

He pulled on a pair of thick gloves from his pack and knelt down by the statue. He met Vishal's dark eyes. The other man nodded. Marietti put his gloved hands on the statue.

Nothing happened.

Their collective sigh of relief echoed through the cave.

Marietti picked it up. "It looks like it's made up of several pieces anyway," he said. "Perhaps it was hidden separately way back when it was created."

He pulled out the flames from behind the dancing Shiva and then unscrewed the god from its pedestal and finally split the base in two.

Vishal pulled some rags from his bag, wrapped up one half of the base along with the flames and handed them to Marietti.

"I will take good care of the other pieces," he said.

Marietti nodded. He trusted the Indian, but he also knew that hard times could change anyone's mind. He needed to ensure that Vishal was never tempted to sell the statue. Himmler's diary had other maps in it, and there were treasures hidden in this land that could be useful now.

He put his hand out and shook Vishal's, meeting the man's eyes. "I know you will," he said. "But there's something else I'd like to talk to you about."

A medical alarm down the hallway interrupted Marietti's dream and he was suddenly back in the present, trapped in the hospital bed years later.

Vishal had taken some of the treasure they found later and used it to start a business empire. His natural ability to charm and his entrepreneurial spirit had taken him into the realm of billionaire. Marietti had returned to the Vatican, handed in his notice and joined ARKANE. He wanted to hunt for artifacts but he didn't want to do it under the auspices of the Vatican anymore.

Nataline had returned to Goa and, God help him, he had gone to her more than once. He missed the cool touch of her hands on his fevered skin now. He missed ... Marietti sighed. He had given her up for his work, like so much else in his life and as regret circled him, he slipped back into unconsciousness.

CHAPTER 12

Agra, India

MORGAN AND JAKE EMERGED from the taxi in front of the public gates of the Taj Mahal complex. They had flown into New Delhi and been driven the 110 kilometers through the night, both grabbing as much sleep as possible on the way. Morgan felt rumpled from the long flight, her limbs cramped, but she also had a sense of excitement about seeing the mausoleum again.

It was still dark, a few hours before dawn, but already the courtyard thronged with vendors. Some laid out postcards and t-shirts alongside snow globes and brass replicas of the famous dome. Others cooked street food, the sizzling of onions and turmeric filling the air with a heady tang.

"Here, madam," an enthusiastic young man shouted, as he noticed the foreigners arrive. He ran over with his arms full of cheap souvenirs which he brandished in front of them. Morgan was swiftly reminded that the sense of personal space in India differed from the West. He soon gave up at their indifference.

But there was something here that Morgan definitely wanted. She took some small rupee notes and bought cups of chai from one of the sellers, handing one to Jake. The tea was rich with buffalo milk, sweet with sugar, and spicy with cardamom and cinnamon.

"That *is* good," Jake said, and went back for a second helping. He returned with two more cups and some paratha bread and they stood in the semi-darkness, listening to the bustle around them.

"I could drink this all the time," Morgan said as the hot drink revived her. "Chai is one of my favorite things about India."

"I got these too," Jake said. He pulled out a little tub filled with syrupy dough balls. "Gulab jamun. Like sticky toffee sweeties."

Morgan dipped her fingers in and pulled one of the balls out, lifting it to her mouth quickly as the syrup dripped to the ground. It was an explosion of sweetness, almost too much, and she swallowed it down in a moment of extreme pleasure.

"These are Ganesha's favorites," she said and reached for another one. "The elephant-headed god always has one hand full of them."

As they munched happily in a moment of simple pleasure, Jake checked his watch. "Martin said that we should be meeting a professor near the main gate soon," he said. "Apparently, he works here occasionally and has out-of-hours access. Let's head over there."

They walked to the public gate and stood waiting in the semi-darkness. It was impossible to see the famous view of the dome from their position, as the visitor had to walk through a courtyard before reaching the iconic mausoleum. But the area in front of the gate was abuzz with activity and they had plenty of life to watch as they waited.

It would only get busier as the day wore on. Agra was notorious for overcrowding and, at peak times, the crush of tourists in the heat of the sun was unbearable. The smell of sweaty bodies and the shout of tour guides made peaceful contemplation of its beauty impossible. India was often best before the crowds and Morgan was glad that Martin had sorted out a way in before the place officially opened. She looked at her watch.

If the professor turned up, of course.

It was best to breathe and adjust to Indian time. Things would happen when they happened. She sipped the last of her chai as a tinge of pink appeared above the horizon and the black sky turned to shades of indigo.

A few minutes later, a soft voice came from behind the gate.

"Mr Timber?"

Jake and Morgan turned to see a thin, older Indian man beckoning to them from inside. He smoked a hand-rolled *bidi* cigarette, sucking on it as he waved. He wore a faded green jacket with a Nehru collar over dark jeans. Both were ill-fitting and made him look like he'd lost a lot of weight recently.

"This way, please." They followed him to a smaller side gate and went inside. He walked away quickly, gesturing for them to follow. "Hurry. We must get away from the view of the gate."

The man only stopped when they were out of sight of those on the other side. He stubbed the end of the *bidi* out and placed the butt in a nearby bin. He adjusted his jacket and held out his hand in a proper manner.

"I'm sorry to be so hasty, but there are watchers at the gate." They shook hands as he continued. "Some report to people who would not approve of your visit. I'm Professor Chetan Palekar from Delhi University, employed briefly by your good company to show you inside the Taj. I'm an expert in Mughal architecture." He pointed to the next archway. "This way please and you may see the beginnings of the sunrise before the tourist horde."

They walked through the arch and suddenly, there it was.

The mausoleum of Shah Jahan's beloved wife with the iconic dome and four tall minarets, reflected in a long pool of water and flanked by manicured gardens. Morgan gazed up at it, silhouetted against the last stars of night. The early morning mist shrouded the edifice, but every second the sun rose higher and revealed more of its grandeur.

Morgan had stood right here with Elian many years ago but strangely, she didn't feel his loss so heavily now, just a sense of how different she was. She had been someone else back then, caught up in ideology, ignorant of so much that ARKANE had revealed of the world beneath the headlines.

"A teardrop on the cheek of eternity," she whispered.

Chetan nodded. "Yes, indeed. As described by Rabindranath Tagore, one of India's greatest poets. The Taj is a World Heritage Site and one of the jewels in India's architectural crown."

They stood in silence for a moment, then a clang came from behind them as if someone else had come through the gate.

Chetan looked back in alarm, but there was no one there.

"Come," he said, a worried furrow in his brow. "We must get inside before they open the gates. We can't be found here."

He pointed at a footpath off to the side, shielded by a row of cyprus trees so as to avoid the walk down the main boulevard in view of anyone else arriving. Chetan scurried ahead, his long legs striding away and Jake and Morgan walked quickly after him.

"Do you think we should be expecting company?" Morgan whispered. After the unexpected attack in Geneva, Martin had arranged for weapons to be issued on the military flight over, but they had hoped to be in and out of the Taj before anyone knew they were even there. They did not want to be caught with guns at one of India's most important monuments.

"I hope not." Jake nodded towards Chetan. "Because he's not going to be much use in any kind of fight."

As they drew closer to the mausoleum, the complexity of the building became evident. The ivory-colored marble was inlaid with ornate designs of flowers and Arabic calligraphy, the green, red and black highlighted with semi-precious stones. Although the building was heavy marble and anchored to the earth, it seemed light and airy, with decoration lifting the architecture into the realm of art.

Chetan led them under the vaulted archway into the main chamber. Morgan and Jake pulled torches from their packs and shone them around, illuminating the twin sarcophagi before them, surrounded by an intricately designed metal barrier.

"This is the tomb of Mumtaz Mahal," Chetan said. "She was the beloved wife of the Mughal Emperor Shah Jahan and she died during the birth of their fourteenth child. It was built in the mid-seventeenth century and it is said that over 20,000 artisans worked on it."

Morgan looked up into the vaulted dome overhead and then played the torch around the corners of the chamber. It was smaller than she remembered and there were no obvious places to hide a piece of a sculpture, especially that of a Hindu god. This was a Muslim tomb, after all.

Jake was clearly thinking the same thing as he peered through the grating at the sarcophagi of Shah Jahan and his beloved wife. They were beautifully decorated with flowers but otherwise they were quite plain, with none of the embellishments of Catholic monarchs in Europe.

"I don't think we're going to find anything here," he said, disappointment in his voice.

"Oh, but these are not the real tombs," Chetan said.

"So where are the real ones?" Morgan asked. "That's what we need to see."

"Oh no, no." Chetan shook his head. "That's impossible. I can't take you down there."

Suddenly, they heard shouting from outside.

Raised voices spoke quickly in Hindi and the flash of torchlight from outside pierced the interior of the mausoleum.

CHAPTER 13

MORGAN PULLED OUT HER gun and moved to the side of the main door. Jake slipped silently to the other side. Chetan huddled behind the tomb and crouched near the floor, closing his eyes as if that would make everything go away.

The three of them stood still and silent for a moment as they listened. It was soon clear that the noise was only the jovial banter of security guards doing their rounds before opening up to the public for the day.

As the sound faded away, Jake walked around the tomb and pulled Chetan to his feet.

"We need to see the real tomb."

Chetan nodded, his forehead beaded with sweat at the near-discovery. "This way." He walked quickly over to a side panel behind the tombs. He slid his hand along the marble design, touching the intricate carvings gently as he searched for the entrance. "It's been a long time since I was last here."

There was an audible click and a metal handle popped out from the marble. Chetan tugged it to reveal a door and stone steps spiraling down into darkness.

Morgan shone her torch ahead and walked down into the lower level of the tomb as the men followed behind. The room was simple and stark, with two marble sarcophagi, the Emperor's bigger and grander than his beloved wife's. The walls were a fine patchwork of marble blocks in hues of pink and grey, the fine grain polished to perfection. It was cool and the air smelled of a light incense. Not a bad place to spend eternity.

She spun around and shone her torch at the walls, but there looked to be nowhere obvious to hide a piece of the sculpture. She shook her head.

"Another dead end." Her voice echoed in the chamber. "There's clearly nothing here."

"What exactly are you looking for?" Chetan asked. "Your employer said only to show you around."

Jake pulled out his smart phone to reveal a picture of the Shiva Nataraja sculpture. "A piece of a sculpture like this," he said.

Chetan paled and his hand flew to his throat in alarm.

"You come here looking for Shiva." He shook his head in despair, his eyes bulging in fear. "I might as well tell you this, but there are those who would deny it and consider it slander. The Taj Mahal is dear to the nation, a flashpoint for emotion." He took a deep breath and continued as he paced up and down in the small tomb. "Some say that this land was not empty when the Taj was created and there are aspects of the building that are several hundred years older. There are rumors that an ancient Hindu temple lies beneath, dedicated to Shiva."

"It's not unusual for kings and conquerors to build over existing holy places," Jake said. "Most of Europe's great churches are built on originally pagan sites. So why is it such a big deal if it happened here?"

Morgan leaned against the cool stone of Mumtaz's tomb.

"The history of Muslims and Hindus in India is complicated and at times, very bloody," she whispered. "So I understand, Chetan. In Israel, there are those who still dispute the ownership of a particular piece of land thousands of years ago, as if that should affect who owns it today. These ancient grudges last a long time."

"But essentially there could be a temple to Shiva underneath," Jake said. "Which means the sculpture piece could still be here. So how do we get to it?"

* * *

Asha Kapoor leaned against the window of the helicopter as they dropped down into Agra, soaring over the city towards the Taj Mahal. She dialed a number on her phone.

"We'll be landing in the Taj Gardens," she said with a tone of authority. "Make sure the public aren't let in until I leave."

Her contact in the tourism department would be well paid for the service, and they would have the time they needed to locate the sculpture piece. Money was useful at times like these, but ultimately it was ephemeral. She was set on a greater goal, a legacy that would last longer than the business her father had created. Asha's heart beat faster at the possibility that she might soon hold the third piece in her hands. The Aghori would be pleased with her and they would be one step closer to the sacrifice.

The helicopter hovered over the manicured lawn of the Taj Mahal garden, its rotors beating the air as it descended. Branches of surrounding trees were whipped into a frenzy at the sudden chop of wind, but as the helicopter engine shut down, calm was restored to the garden again.

Asha climbed out of the helicopter, bending low as she walked quickly towards the mausoleum. Two of her bodyguards followed along, their weapons tucked away as they dragged another man between them.

Gopan had written a book on the existence of a Hindu temple under the Taj Mahal. He had gone into hiding when the book had brought him death threats, but Asha's hackers had found him in little time and they had picked him up on the way from Bangladesh. If her father had left a piece of the

Shiva statue at the Muslim Taj Mahal, surely it would make sense that it be located where this fabled Shiva temple was.

Now Gopan would have the chance to prove his conspiracy theory for real. If he was wrong … well, there was a faster way out of the helicopter to the ground below.

They reached the steps of the mausoleum and Asha turned.

"So, how do we get into this ancient temple?" she said.

She stepped closer to Gopan. He was young, maybe twenty-five, with a poor excuse for a mustache and a straggly beard. Dried blood crusted around his nose and his right eyebrow where a well-placed blow had persuaded him to join the search.

"I … it …" Sweat beaded on his upper lip and his breath came fast as he struggled for words.

"There's no need to be scared," Asha said softly. She pulled a handkerchief out, dabbed at his bloody face and then motioned for the bodyguards to let the man go. They dropped their hands and stepped back, silent in obedience. "Your book was so brilliant and I need your help to find this ancient temple. Will you help me?"

Gopan took a deep breath. "It is only a theory," he said. "We might not find anything."

Asha gave a light smile. "I think you'd better try finding something. After all, I've come a long way for this."

Gopan pointed up towards the main entrance. "Then we must go into the main mausoleum and down to the place where the real tombs are. My sources say that the entrance is down in the crypt."

Asha began to walk up the steps.

* * *

Below in the tomb, Chetan vehemently shook his head. "This ancient Shiva temple is only rumored to exist," he said. "And I don't know how we could find it anyway."

"There must be something here." Jake began to search the small tomb again, playing his torch over the walls as he searched for hidden seams that might hide another entrance.

Morgan stood for a moment and watched him search. Something was bothering her. Something about the history of the Taj.

She pulled up the notes from Martin on her smart phone and skimmed the information about the CERN statue and the Taj Mahal. A moment later, she found what she was looking for.

"Look at this," she said. "The same man, Vishal Kapoor, was involved in both the UNESCO World Heritage Site transformation project of the Taj Mahal and the CERN statue. In his early career, he worked on archaeological digs including some for the Vatican. He had to have hidden the piece." She turned to Chetan. "So what was changed here when the Taj became a UNESCO site? Did they make any structural changes?"

"Maybe so." Chetan waggled his head in that Indian way of saying maybe yes or maybe no. "I think they shored up the side closest to the Yamuna River in case of flooding for safety reasons. There was some other minor work, but that would be the most significant. They had many experts here then. Perhaps this man was able to access the old shrine – if it existed at all."

Jake turned and walked to the northern wall of the tomb. "The river is on this side."

Morgan joined him and together they examined the wall more closely. They both ran their hands over the intricate inlaid marble design in the same way Chetan had done upstairs.

The seconds ticked by.

"There's nothing here," Morgan said with disappointment. "Perhaps the sculpture piece was hidden in some other part of the complex. There's more to the Taj Mahal than just the tomb."

"Give me one more minute," Jake said. He bent to the floor and began to examine the flagstones.

* * *

Asha walked into the mausoleum. The dawn penetrated inside now and she could see the cool gleam of the marble tombs in the half-light. She leaned close to the metal grating and gazed in at the two lovers, lying side by side. She had read of Mumtaz Mahal and how she was both wife and mother, but also a trusted companion of the Emperor. She was the equal of Shah Jahan and their marriage had been testament to how much a true partnership could achieve. Asha had once wished for someone to share her life, but the men her father had suggested were weak, with none of the ambition that burned inside of her. She would never be buried in a tomb like this, she would never be loved as Mumtaz had been, but she intended to be remembered for far longer.

She turned to Gopan.

"Where now?"

He walked over to a side panel and ran his hands along the wall. "The way down to the lower tomb is here." His face paled and he pulled his hands away in shock.

"What is it?" Asha asked.

"The door is open," Gopan said. "Someone else is here."

CHAPTER 14

DOWN IN THE CRYPT, Morgan and Jake froze at the sounds coming from above.

"There's no other way out," Chetan whispered, his voice wavering. "And I left the door open. They'll know we're here."

Morgan pulled her gun out and pointed it towards the steps leading down from above.

"Help Jake look," she said softly. "If there is a shrine, now's the time to find it. We can't have a shootout in the Taj Mahal."

Chetan fell to his knees and crawled along the marble slabs, sweeping his fingers across the stones as Jake worked his way from the opposite end.

"Here," Jake said suddenly. "There's a handle. We can pull this slab out. Help me, Chetan."

Together the men lifted one of the smaller marble blocks from the floor, revealing a dark hole below. Jake shone his torch in. It was about six feet deep and there was water and rubble in the bottom where a partially collapsed tunnel doglegged away from the access point.

"It doesn't look too good," Jake whispered. Morgan turned to look briefly, tearing her eyes from the staircase.

"We have to try," she said. "There's no cover in here. We're screwed if it comes to a firefight." In the moment of quiet, they heard the door creak open upstairs. "I'm going."

She clambered down into the hole and Chetan half fell down after her. Jake came last and pulled the slab over again. Just as he slotted it into place, he saw torchlight flicker on the spiral stairs. It wouldn't take those following long to find the entrance, and there was no way of blocking it from below.

They had to hurry.

* * *

Asha and Gopan followed the two bodyguards down the stairs into the tomb. The men reached the bottom and swung their torches around, tracking the beam with their guns.

"It's clear," one of them said. "There's no one here."

Asha walked into the middle of the room. The atmosphere felt unsettled somehow. The cool air had been disturbed. But there looked to be no exit … or was there?

She turned to Gopan.

"How do we get to this ancient Shiva shrine?"

"I … I don't know, madam. Truly, I don't." He grabbed hold of the nearest sarcophagus and leaned against it as he shook with fear. "My sources say it is under here but there's no telling how to get to it."

Asha walked closer to the man. She gestured to one of the bodyguards and he handed her a kukri – a Tibetan machete – from his belt. Gopan's eyes bulged at the sight of the weapon, its blade glinting in the torchlight.

Asha swung it around in two hands, adept in her weapon skills.

"I follow Kali, in her Destroyer aspect," she said. "You know the goddess?"

Gopan nodded.

"Tell me what you know." Asha took a step towards him. The blade flashed before her, torchlight flickering over the silver edge.

"She is garlanded with the skulls of the dead and holds a severed head in one hand." Gopan's voice shook with terror.

"She holds a knife, too," Asha said softly. "The weapon with which she dispatches her sacrifice."

Gopan backed away, his hands out in supplication.

"No, please."

He found himself up against the wall of the tomb, hemmed in by marble.

"If you don't know where the shrine is, then you only have one purpose remaining." Asha nodded at her bodyguards.

They grabbed Gopan and lifted him onto the sarcophagus of Shah Jahan. He struggled and screamed but they held him down as Asha stalked towards her prey. Her pulse pounded and she could feel the incarnation of the goddess rise inside her, hungering to feed.

The shrine would be found, but only through offering a sacrifice. The Aghori often found answers in blood. Perhaps she would be able to read it, too.

She stood at the side of the sarcophagus and lifted the kukri above her head. One of the bodyguards tugged Gopan's head back, revealing his bare throat.

Asha said a prayer to the goddess and asked for her guidance.

She brought the weapon down.

A dull thunk resounded in the marble tomb and Gopan's head was severed from his torso. The bodyguard stepped back from the corpse and the head rolled off onto the floor, its eyes wide and mouth open, frozen in a final scream.

Blood pulsed from the dead man's flesh and ran across the floor. Asha watched the blood trail as it trickled down into the seams of the marble slabs. Then she noticed it pooling around one in particular and she smiled. The goddess had shown the way.

"There," she said to the bodyguards. "Pull that up."

* * *

Morgan ran down the tunnel as Chetan and Jake followed close behind. She had to duck her head so it didn't touch the low ceiling which meant the men behind would be bent over even further. She could hear the professor panting as he struggled to keep up but they couldn't stop. Whoever was behind them wouldn't be delayed for long.

She shone her torch ahead to illuminate the simple structure that held the earth up above their heads. Wooden pillars shored up the sides of the tunnel. It smelled of mold and some of the wood was rotten and splintered from the river water that had seeped in over time. Morgan splashed through muddy puddles as she ran, and with every step she hoped that the tunnel would end up somewhere useful.

A minute later her torch flickered across an entranceway and she emerged into a chamber. The tunnel from the Taj Mahal had clearly been added more recently, but this place looked to be much older than the mausoleum above. Stone slabs had been used to create a circular space, the low ceiling held up by a large pillar. The atmosphere was damp and warm, a primal place where life could grow, and yet the stones were stark and deep grey, like the skies before monsoon rain. On one side of the chamber there was a lingam – a short pillar of stone representing the god Shiva in the phallic principle, the creative energy of God. On the far side, there was another tunnel leading away towards the river.

Chetan and Jake emerged from the tunnel behind her.

"Oh my goodness," Chetan sighed. "It really does exist."

"This place looks pretty old," Jake said as he walked around the main pillar, his eyes flicking over the empty space. "But we really need to find that sculpture piece. It must have been put here much later if indeed it was placed here by Vishal Kapoor during the UNESCO renovations."

Morgan bent down to the lingam and placed both hands upon it. The stone was cool but not as cold as she had expected, as if a latent warmth flowed through it from the earth. It was smooth and she felt an urge to rest her cheek against it, to stop for a moment in this calm place and just breathe.

She smiled at the thought, as she realized why this more austere representation of the deity made her feel more at home. The synagogues she had been brought up with in Israel had no graven images and this place reminded her of that simplicity of faith. She felt more at home here than in Catholic churches with their tortured saints, or in the more elaborate Hindu shrines with their colorful incarnations of the various gods. In contrast, this stone was elemental.

She ran her hands down the sides of the lingam to the base and then looked behind it. There was an oilskin package tucked flush against the wall.

"There's something here." She leaned in and pulled it out. The package was waxy and crinkled, but there was something hard inside.

She squatted on the floor and Jake aimed his torch at the package as Morgan gingerly pulled the edges apart.

"Careful," he said. "We know there's something strange about these pieces, so don't touch it."

Morgan used the side of her own torch to push the edges of the package fully open. She caught a glimpse of bronze in the torchlight before the sculpture piece was fully revealed.

It was the god himself, frozen in his cosmic dance. The detail was exquisite, each finger perfectly formed, each snake undulating around him, a calm smile on his face, even as he looked into the end of the world.

"This is what you came for?" Chetan asked. "I see it is Lord Shiva, but what–"

His words were cut off as a thump echoed down the tunnel.

Whoever was following them had found the entrance.

Morgan quickly wrapped the sculpture piece again and put it inside her pack.

"We'll have to take a chance that the tunnel will get us out of here." Jake pointed his torch into the blackness ahead.

Morgan again took the lead and ran into the tunnel. It

angled upwards and as they drew closer to the river, the puddles turned into a more constant water flow and soon the water lapped around her ankles.

Suddenly she could see light ahead and she waded towards it, dragging her feet out of the mud, squelching with every step.

"Come on," she called back to Chetan and Jake behind her. "We're almost there."

They scrambled from the tunnel and emerged onto the bank of the Yamuna River at the northeast corner of the Taj Mahal compound. Dawn had broken and the early sun sparkled on the river. On the opposite bank, women were already out washing and people performed *puja* and yoga stretches on the riverbank, the daily rituals of the morning.

"We can go east from here into the wetlands national park," Jake said, as he pointed towards the edge of a green oasis. "It's a protected bird sanctuary and wild enough that there will be ample cover. It will be hard to follow us and we can hide in there while we arrange transport out of here."

Chetan bent over and wheezed, his breath ragged as he tried to recover.

"I cannot ... go any further ... I'll make my own way from here."

Morgan grabbed his arm. "No, you have to come with us. You could be in danger."

The professor shook her off and stood tall.

"I have friends here in the complex. I'll head back up to the main mausoleum and into the administration area to clean up. I'll be fine. You go ahead. Quickly now."

Jake looked back down the tunnel. "We don't have time to argue," he said. "We have to go."

"Please, Chetan," Morgan tried one last time. "We can protect you."

The professor spun on his heel and pulled a *bidi* cigarette from his pocket with a shaking hand as he stalked away. Morgan stared after him for a moment. Short of dragging him off, they couldn't stop him. But they couldn't stay any longer either.

Morgan and Jake ran together along the muddy bank and ducked into the wetlands foliage as soon as they could.

As they entered the green perimeter, Morgan turned and looked back. She could just make out Chetan's slight figure climbing the riverbank back up towards the mausoleum. She didn't want to leave him behind, but they had to get the sculpture piece away from here.

She turned and jogged after Jake until they lost sight of the river, cloaked by the thick protection of the national park.

* * *

Asha hurried through the tunnel flanked by her body-guards, one ahead shining his torch to light the way and the other behind. She would have to call her contact in the Taj administration to clear up the mess in the tomb once they were back up top. She chuckled a little to think of the surprise they would have. But whatever she found down here, if indeed there was an earlier Hindu shrine, it would all be covered up and declared a conspiracy theory anyway. She wasn't worried about any bad press. But she was worried about who had found this place first. There were footprints in the mud and the air was disturbed. Had they found what she herself sought?

"Here, madam," the bodyguard in front said as they emerged into a round chamber buttressed by stone walls. A Shiva lingam was the only feature in the ancient space and Asha knew that the Aghori would appreciate its austerity.

She noticed a patch on the floor where the earth had been recently disturbed. Something had been found here, but somehow she knew it was gone with those who had been here just moments before.

"You." She pointed at one of the bodyguards. "Run up that tunnel as fast as you can. Detain anyone you find and I will follow."

The bodyguard ran ahead, disappearing into the dark. Asha followed behind, relishing the exercise. It was good to be hunting, and she was so close to finding another piece.

She could feel it.

Minutes later, Asha emerged onto the riverbank, her feet muddy and her jeans wet with river water. The bodyguard was out of sight, but she could hear his voice threatening someone nearby and the answering cries of his victim.

"Please, don't hurt me. I don't know anything. I was just out walking before my shift."

Asha clambered up the riverbank back onto the grounds of the Taj Mahal complex. Her bodyguard held a tall thin man by the scruff of his shirt, fist pulled back as he threatened a blow.

"If you were just walking the grounds, why are your trousers wet with river water?" Asha said as she walked closer. Her eyes scanned over the man. "And why do you have earth on your shirt?"

The man's eyes widened in fear. He had been in the tunnel. She knew it.

"I ... I was just–"

Asha nodded at the bodyguard. His fist pounded the side of the man's face and knocked him to the ground, then he kicked the man hard in the stomach with heavy boots.

The man moaned and curled on the ground. Asha walked towards him and pulled the kukri from her belt. Its blade was still stained with the blood of sacrifice.

"Look at me," she whispered. The man looked up to see the bloody blade. "You *will* tell me what you're doing here." Her voice was soft.

He bent his head and his shoulders slumped.

"I will tell you everything, madam."

CHAPTER 15

MORGAN AND JAKE TRAMPED through the wetlands and into the forest, sticking close to the cover of the tamarind and cypress trees. Birds trilled at their approach and the air was cool out of the sun. As they walked, Jake held up his phone to try and get a signal, but the reception was patchy.

"If we can get a pickup," he said, "we'll get the sculpture piece to the ARKANE headquarters in Delhi. I know someone there who will help us on the quiet."

"Maybe we can find out who has been following us," Morgan said, her mind still on Chetan.

"Here we go." Jake stopped and dialed, providing details of where they were. The call finished and he turned to Morgan. "They're sending a local driver to take us back to Delhi. We just need to get to the main road further east."

They walked in companionable silence through the lush green national park, one of the few places in Agra protected from the development that had turned the rest of the city into an urban sprawl. The sculpture piece weighed heavy in Morgan's pack. Now they had one of the pieces, there was no way the whole thing could be put together again. But she wondered at Marietti's involvement and why he had protected its secret for so long. What was it capable of?

They soon reached the road to find an air-conditioned taxi waiting for them. They climbed in and the driver handed them bottles of water, frowning only slightly at their disheveled appearance.

"Welcome," he said with a smile. "It will only be a few hours to Delhi on the express highway. Please relax and enjoy your trip."

It was nearing lunchtime as they hit the outskirts of Delhi and the traffic was pretty much as expected for the gigantic Indian city. The sound of horns and Bollywood music permeated the cab even through the windows. The highway soon narrowed into smaller roads as they wound their way towards the central area.

"I am to drop you at the Jantar Mantar," the driver said. "Is this correct?"

Morgan looked at Jake, a question in her eyes. She had never been here before and she was still relatively new as an ARKANE agent, whereas Jake had been on global missions for years. He hadn't spoken of any past experiences in India, but then, they still knew so little about each other.

"Yes," he said. "By the main entrance will be fine."

They emerged into the heat of the midday sun in front of the Jantar Mantar, a huge complex of architectural astronomy instruments completed in 1724 by one of the Maharajas. The usual rush of merchants and beggars crowded about them as Morgan and Jake walked towards the entrance.

A man in a white lungi sat cross-legged on the ground playing a wooden pipe. A woven basket lay in front of him and a small cobra peeked its head out, undulating to the music.

"A real snake charmer," Morgan said as they passed. "I thought perhaps they were an urban myth."

"No fangs," Jake smiled. "All the tourists love a good snake charming. Come on, the ARKANE entrance is inside, away from the hordes."

They walked past the giant instruments, the terracotta shapes incongruous against the backdrop of towering office blocks that had sprung up in the wake of India's phenomenal economic growth.

"We're only a short distance from Connaught Place," Jake said. "The former location of the headquarters of the British Raj. The ARKANE office here was established at the same time as the British Empire. After Independence, ARKANE went underground but even as some of the biggest companies in India developed buildings here, we still retained a foothold. This country has more than enough mystery to keep the local agents busy."

He led Morgan to the very end of the complex, where a shabby breeze-block building sat, ignored by those who only had eyes for the ancient monument. It looked like a disused electrical plant or an abandoned guards' room.

Jake pushed open the door to reveal a storeroom with discarded garden equipment and piles of old boxes. Morgan stepped inside and as she closed the door behind her, the room shifted and changed. Lasers flashed from the walls and scanned their bodies. After a moment there was an audible clunking noise.

"This way." Jake opened a cupboard to reveal a lift inside.

They descended quickly and Morgan felt her ears pop. As in Oxford and London, the ARKANE offices were deep below the earth. It occurred to her that she could really do with some sunlight after way too long underground today.

She pushed that thought aside and focused instead on Trafalgar Square and how that had been breached. Were they putting this place in danger by bringing the sculpture piece inside?

At the bottom, they emerged into a plain room. A door opened in front of them and a stunning woman stepped out. Her long dark hair cascaded to a slim waist, and her tailored burgundy trouser suit did nothing to hide her curvaceous figure. Perfect eyebrows arched over dark intelligent eyes that fixed on Jake.

"It's been a long time," she said, walking over. Jake embraced her and the woman's hand lingered on the nape of his neck. The familiar touch made Morgan suspect that there was something more than professional between them.

The woman stepped back. "I'm glad you're here at last, even under these difficult circumstances." She turned to Morgan and held out a slim hand, her manicured nails dark with indigo polish. "I'm Shilpa Aggarwal, Director of ARKANE here in India."

"Dr Morgan Sierra." Morgan shook Shilpa's hand and met the woman's cool gaze, suddenly aware of the muddy clothing they wore and the smell of the river wafting off them. "I'm Jake's partner."

Shilpa turned back to Jake. "There are rumors that you're working on something unsanctioned. People higher up are asking questions."

"We need your help," he said. "And we have to keep it quiet."

Shilpa nodded slowly. "What can I do?"

Morgan pulled the wrapped package from her bag.

"It's another piece of the Shiva Nataraja sculpture," Jake said. "We presume it's part of the same statue as the piece taken in the Trafalgar Square bombing, but we need it verified. We won't be here long. We don't want a repeat of London, but we could use your help with where the next piece might be." He pointed down at his disheveled clothing. "Plus we could use a shower and some new clothes."

"Of course." Shilpa's eyes flickered over Jake's body and Morgan pushed down a flush of jealousy. What Jake did in the shower was no concern of hers, as long as he hurried up so they could get on with the mission.

Shilpa led them through to the ARKANE labs, the setup similar to London with self-contained rooms where ancient artifacts were investigated as to their occult properties. Morgan wished they had more time here. There were mysteries in this country she would love to research further.

But there was never enough time.

They walked through into a changing area.

"I'll leave you to freshen up," Shilpa said. "And I'll get someone in the lab to look at the sculpture piece immediately and verify its provenance." She held up a hand. "Don't worry. We'll keep it quiet and won't log anything official."

Morgan handed over the oilskin package and Shilpa walked from the room.

Jake began to strip off his clothes, a cheeky smile playing around his lips. Morgan turned away, not trusting herself to stay so close to him, and headed into the female showers.

She sighed with pleasure as the hot water poured down upon her. It had already been a very long day and it was only lunchtime. She scrubbed the river mud from her skin and it swirled down the drain in grey trails. Her fingers lingered on the scars at her side and she thought of Jake and the scars on his body sustained at the bone church. Was Shilpa touching those scars even now?

Don't be an idiot. She shook her head. *Enough already.*

She got dressed quickly and walked to the communal area to find that lunch had been laid out for them. A number of small dishes filled with perfectly made vegetarian food were arranged next to a pile of roti bread. Morgan's stomach rumbled and she gratefully tucked into a gobi masala, a tangy cauliflower dish that exploded with flavor in her mouth.

Jake emerged a few minutes later, his hair wet from the shower.

"That looks good," he said, sitting down next to her and tucking in. He smelled spicy and fresh and she could feel his body heat next to her. Morgan quashed the innuendo that rose to her lips and they both ate with relish.

The door opened and Shilpa came in. This time her beautiful face was marred with a frown, her expression grave.

"We've run the sculpture piece through the lab and the radioactive signature is the same as the piece taken from the London vault. It's also a match to a secret cave discovered at

Ellora. We suspect the original sculpture was found there. I've been on the phone to Martin in London and it seems that Marietti was in India in the '80s."

"So that's two pieces we know about," Jake said. "But there are still two more. I'd feel more confident if we had another piece. Do you have any ideas as to where to search next?"

Shilpa shook her head. "We're still looking for any other artifacts or places that resonate with that radioactive signature. But it will take time."

Morgan sat silently for a moment. She hesitated to bring a friend into the mission but they were out of ideas.

"There is someone I can ask," she said. "Someone who knew Marietti long ago."

CHAPTER 16

FATHER BEN COSTANZA WALKED through the narrow gate from St Giles and stepped into the heart of Blackfriars, a Dominican Permanent Private Hall of the University of Oxford. Despite the ever-changing matters of faith and internecine squabbles of the Church, not to mention the malleable face of the university, this small quad was one of the constants in Ben's life. Along with his morning constitutional walk around the University Parks, of course, and a neat espresso from Taylors on the corner of Little Clarendon Street. He hummed a few bars from Mozart's Benedictus, a smile on his face as he recalled the early-blooming flowers in the park. It was a blessing to have another day in this beautiful city.

Ben rather liked Mondays. Sunday was always a workday if work related to the church, and his still did after all these years. On Mondays he only had one tutorial session with a Ph.D. student studying the history of the Dominican Order in Britain. Ben was a tutor for the Angelicum, the Baccalaureate in Sacred Theology granted by the Pontifical University of St Thomas in Rome. The session wasn't too taxing and he could soon return to his own private study.

But despite the spring in his step, he was feeling the years more heavily these days, made worse by a spiritual weight caused by the rise in religious fundamentalism both in the East and West. He had seen such things before, of course, and time is ever cyclical. People forget the mistakes of the past so soon, but this time he didn't know if he would live to see the end of the cycle.

As a former archaeologist, he mourned the destruction of the ancient city of Palmyra, recently blown up by Islamic State. But then, the religious had always destroyed what they called paganism. The Christian edict to destroy the great library of Alexandria back in 391 AD was one order he particularly regretted. The classical knowledge destroyed there and later repressed in Europe by vehement Christians could perhaps have prevented the Dark Ages. Even now, humanity continued to repeat those mistakes. Of course, he had the Bodleian, one of the greatest libraries in the world, here at Oxford University but Ben found himself coveting what had lain within those hallowed walls millennia ago.

He walked across the quad and climbed the stairs towards his office, feeling the arthritis in his knees as he made his way up but refusing to let the pain show on his face. He was determined to keep this room where he could see the rooftops of Oxford. He didn't want one of those dark ground-floor offices but he knew some of the younger lot kept their eye on him, like vultures ready to pounce on the dead. But as long as he continued to be useful, he would find a place here.

His phone buzzed and he pulled it out of his pocket. Ben smiled as he accepted the call from Morgan.

"I heard about the bombing in London," he said. "Anything to do with ARKANE?"

"You know I can't comment on that." He could hear the smile in her voice. "But I do have a case to work on and I'm hoping you might be able to help. You'll need to ransack your memory though, and it's about someone you have issues with."

"Marietti."

Ben's shoulders slumped as he felt the veil of time swirl about him. Marietti was a similar age and their history went

back years, back to the Vatican, back even to the archaeological digs at Ephesus years before. Ben had told Morgan
about the dig where he had met her parents and about his
own forbidden love for her mother, who had died from
breast cancer years ago now.

But Morgan didn't know everything.

Marietti was bound up in Ben's own emotional history
with the Church and at this time in his life, he didn't really
want to dig it all up again. But he had promised Morgan's
mother, Marianne, that he would always help her daughters,
and he saw Marianne's face whenever he looked at her twin
girls. As a priest, he would never have his own children, so
Morgan and her twin sister, Faye, were the closest he would
ever get.

"Of course," he said. "What do you need?"

Ben heard rustling as Morgan shuffled papers.

"We think Marietti found something in India back in the
1980s, a Hindu statue of Shiva Nataraja. It has some kind
of relationship to nuclear energy, but we're unsure of the
details. The statue was broken into pieces and each hidden.
Now someone is trying to put them back together, so we
have to find them first. I wondered if you knew or could find
out anything about Marietti's Indian trip."

"You can't ask him yourself?" Ben said.

"He was injured in the blast and we don't know when
he'll be well enough to speak."

"I'm sorry to hear that. Despite our differences, I still
wish him well. But it's strange that the Vatican was even
involved in a Hindu dig," Ben said. "I do know why Shiva
Nataraja would be associated with nuclear power, though.
There's a fable of a weapon, the Brahmastra, mentioned in
the Mahabharata, the Sanskrit epic of ancient India. The text
influenced Oppenheimer, the American theoretical physi-
cist who helped build the atom bomb. He learned Sanskrit
and cited his visit to India as the most influential occasion

in his life. The scriptures speak of an ancient battle where this weapon decimated entire armies, destroying crowds of warriors along with war elephants, melting their weapons. Hold on a second, I have the text here somewhere."

Ben placed the phone on the table, switched it to speakerphone, and turned to his extensive shelf of books. The spines were well worn but despite the volume of titles, it was organized chaos of a kind. As an expert in interfaith matters, Ben had copies of many ancient texts sacred to different religions. He quickly located a translation of the Mahabharata, pulled it down and flicked through the pages.

"Here we are. It talks of a weapon charged with all the power of the universe. A perpendicular explosion with billowing clouds rising in expanding circles. An incandescent column of smoke and flame as bright as a thousand suns, and the weapon as a messenger of death which reduced all to ashes. As a result of the explosion, people's hair and nails fell out and birds turned white in the air. Food was infected and soldiers had to immerse themselves in water to wash themselves clean of infection."

"It certainly sounds like an atomic bomb and the resulting radioactive poisoning," Morgan said. "We need to find the pieces and stop the weapon being activated. Can you help?"

In Ben's mind, he saw a mushroom cloud above the spires of Oxford that billowed out over the city destroying all in its path. There were secrets he had buried long ago, but now it seemed time to unearth them again. In his long years, many of those who knew of the past had died, and each time, Ben wondered if he would be the last one standing. With Marietti in critical condition, there were few remaining. Perhaps it was time to unearth this mystery.

"Have you ever been to Goa?" he asked.

CHAPTER 17

THE PLANE BANKED AND the wing tipped and for a brief moment, Morgan stared down into the deep blue of the Arabian Sea. Goa was a coastal state, its long beaches famous for white sand, relaxation and escape from the city grind. Despite India's frenetic growth and economic boom, Goa still managed to hold on to a slower pace of life.

Father Ben shifted in his sleep and Morgan pulled the blanket up around him. They had met him in Delhi and flown on to Goa together. He had slept most of the way and Morgan had been loath to disturb him, despite her curiosity about what he knew. Jake was reading, catching up on the history of western India, but they were still unsure as to exactly why they were heading for Goa.

Martin Klein had sorted the flights quickly and discreetly, keen for them to pursue any new leads while he investigated who inside ARKANE was plotting against Marietti. The repair of HQ continued apace and Morgan imagined the vault and its precious contents disappearing under London again. Of course, the conspiracy message boards were going nuts about what was really under Trafalgar Square based on pictures taken just after the blast, and denials by MI6 and other British government agencies only intensified the speculation. Some of the more sensitive projects had been moved to the labs under the Natural History Museum in Oxford, but no doubt it wouldn't be long until the news cycle shifted attention again.

Father Ben stretched and yawned.

"We're almost there," Morgan said softly.

"What time is it?" He pushed his sleeve back to reveal the vintage Rolex he had worn in all the years she had known him.

"It's 2.15pm local time," Morgan said.

Ben shook his head as he wound the hands forward. "I don't think I'll ever get used to jet lag. I'm sure part of my soul is still back in Oxford and it will take a day or so to get here."

He smiled and Morgan noticed the lines on his face had deepened since she had seen him last. Was she responsible for the added stress in his life? She had certainly brought danger for him in the time she had worked with ARKANE, and she had dragged him into some crazy adventures. He had been almost blown up at Blackfriars, burned to death in the Freemasons Grand Lodge of England and now ... well, she didn't even know where this would lead. But since the opening salvo of this mysterious group was to blow up Trafalgar Square, she didn't think it would be a quiet stroll through the backwaters of India.

But Ben knew something about Marietti's early life, and they needed his help.

"It's been many years since I visited Goa," Ben said, as the plane landed and taxied along the runway. His eyes were bright with excitement. "But it has haunted my dreams and I've wanted to return many times."

His words trailed off and Morgan was suddenly glad they could have this time together. Whatever happened, it was worth it for this moment of renewed vigor.

"I guess we're not heading for any of these beaches?" Jake brandished the airline magazine at them. It showed palm trees waving over white sand on the edge of a turquoise ocean.

"This place is more than beaches," Ben said. "It's a

UNESCO World Heritage Site for the Portuguese Catholic monuments. Goa was the capital of the Portuguese Indies from 1565 to 1760, and its convents and churches are protected."

"But what has it got to do with Marietti?" Morgan asked, finally unable to restrain her curiosity any longer.

"You know that he was here on an archaeological dig back in the '80s," Ben said. "But afterwards, he was based here for longer than was strictly necessary. It's unclear what his small team found on the dig – perhaps your mysterious sculpture – but this place was certainly special to him and I've heard that he returned secretly a number of times." Ben smiled, his blue eyes twinkling with mischief. "Elias Marietti is just a man, like any other. Of course, he has been faithful to the Church for many years, but a long time ago, there was someone special in his life. I believe she is still here."

Jake's eyes darkened at this revelation and Morgan wondered what he was thinking. Marietti was like a father to him, but there were clearly so many secrets between them.

After navigating customs, they were soon in a taxi speeding away from the airport towards Velha Goa, the old city. Ben gazed out of the window as they drove through the busy streets, his excitement infectious at the sights.

A group of women walked by in brilliantly-colored saris, saffron and purple, bright pink and yellow, some stitched with gold edging. One woman wore the elaborate clothes of Rajasthan, her skirt embroidered with mirrors. The sunlight flashed in their reflection, each tiny piece of glass catching a different part of street life, as each Hindu incarnation echoed a different part of God.

Harsh exhaust fumes choked the air but underneath, the smell of incense lingered, a sense of ancient faith underlying modern technology. There was a different approach to time in India. Belief in the cycles of creation, destruction and reincarnation meant that waiting a little longer to get anywhere wasn't that important.

Finally, they pulled up in front of the Basilica of Bom Jesus.

Morgan stepped out of the car, grateful to stretch her legs after the long journey. The sun was high, the air tropical, and she could feel a trickle of sweat beading on the small of her back.

She looked up at the facade of the Basilica, the extravagant baroque style incongruous in the heat and verdant green of southern India. It had four towering levels with aspects of red brick and white marble giving the church a distinctly European feel. The first level had a huge door flanked by two smaller entrances, and above that two levels of rectangular and round windows were topped with a heavy sloping roof. A lawn of perfectly clipped green grass surrounded the church and two gardeners watered it while stepping softly in bare feet, heads bent to their work.

"This is where the mortal remains of St Francis Xavier are kept," Ben said. "To some, he is the patron saint of Goa, a man of faith worthy of veneration. To others, his body is a reminder of the dark past of the Portuguese in this area. He requested the Inquisition be brought to India in 1545, and although the records are lost, it's clear that thousands died here, burned alive at auto-da-fé. They forbade the practice of Hinduism and persecuted Sephardic Jews who lived here too." Ben shook his head. "I'm not proud of what the Church did back then, and I'm not surprised that few wish to honor that past. But there are many of faith who love this country and some who try and correct the sins of the past. Nataline is one of them." He pointed to the entrance. "Let's go and find her."

Jake led the way while Morgan helped Ben across the lawn at a slower pace. She could feel how thin he was beneath his cotton shirt and she squeezed his arm gently. "I'm glad you're here," she said. "We need you. Marietti was so secretive about his past."

"For good reason," Ben said as they entered the Basilica.

The interior was spacious with high ceilings, the wide windows and cream walls lending the light a buttery tone. The main altar was a wall of gold with paintings of angels singing Gloria to God.

Tourists crowded around one of the side altars, a gigantic Florentine mausoleum with ornate carvings of cherubs and stars. The body of St Francis, believed to be incorrupt and still fresh after nearly 500 years, lay inside a casket within the mausoleum.

But they hadn't come all this way to see the dead.

A security guard stood at the side of the shrine. Ben shuffled over and Morgan smiled to see him emphasize the stoop of age. He put out a frail hand to touch the man's sleeve, as if he needed support. The guard looked down with concern.

"Perhaps you could help me, my son," he said. "I'm looking for Sister Nataline. Is she here today?"

The young man nodded.

"She works in the soup kitchen," he said, in heavily accented English. "You'll probably find her out back."

Ben led Morgan and Jake out of the church and onto the lawn again.

"I'm not surprised she's still here," he said. "It's beautiful, a good place to spend one's later years. I can feel my arthritis improving already."

Jake grinned. "So Sister Nataline is a nun?"

Ben nodded. "But back then, when Marietti was first here, she was an assistant on the archaeological dig. She became a nun later, after he left India. Let's walk around to the kitchen."

They found the soup kitchen area easily, marked by the long line of hungry people outside. More emerged from the tiny doorway with bowls of dahl and rice and sat to eat it on the grass.

They waited until the crowd thinned and then entered the kitchen. It bustled with energy and several nuns stood behind the counters washing dishes and serving food to latecomers. One of the women caught Morgan's eye. She wore a light blue habit, her hair covered with a wimple. Her bearing was almost regal, her back straight and she was clearly of mixed race origin by her light caramel skin. Age only seemed to intensify her delicate features and she was still beautiful. She turned as they entered. Her dark eyes narrowed as she looked more closely at Ben.

She put down her dishcloth and walked to greet them.

"You're welcome here," she said with a humble smile, "but you can find places to eat in the tourist area down the road. This is our charitable kitchen for the poor."

"Are you Sister Nataline?" Ben asked. The nun nodded.

Jake pulled out his smart phone, tapped it and then turned it to show her. Her eyes widened and her hand flew to cover her mouth.

"We'd like to talk to you about this man," Jake said. "Do you recognize him?"

Nataline reached out with one hand and took the phone, zooming in with her fingertips to examine the face more carefully. Her eyes darkened as she smiled and Morgan read a secret history there.

"Of course." Nataline's voice was musical, lighter now. "It's been a long time and we're both old now, but I could never forget Elias."

"Is there somewhere we can talk in private?" Morgan asked.

Nataline led them away from the kitchen to a manicured herb garden, sheltered from the sun by a sailcloth tethered by strong rope, a simple yet effective shade. It smelled of rosemary and thyme, and the soft buzz of insects filled the air.

"We grow these herbs for the kitchen," she said, as they

sat down around a small garden table. "I come to think sometimes and it seems appropriate to talk here of the past. How is Elias?"

"I'm so sorry, but there was an explosion and he was badly hurt," Morgan explained. "The attackers took something, a statue of Shiva Nataraja." Jake pulled up the image of the complete sculpture on his phone and showed her.

Nataline paled.

"I didn't ever expect to hear of that again," she whispered. "I thought I would take its secret to my grave. Elias promised that I could walk away, that I would not have to bear the burden, and yet, here you are." She shook her head. "Perhaps we cannot escape the deeds of our past."

"What can you tell us about the statue?" Jake asked.

"Elias found a Nazi map that pointed to a certain cave system where a weapon might be found. I had my doubts." She smiled. "I was young and cynical back then. But in the cave I saw–"

Before she could continue, a scream rang out across the garden.

A volley of shots cracked through the air from beyond the Basilica.

Jake jumped up and both he and Morgan drew their weapons. They spun around, scanning for danger.

"We have to go," Morgan said. "This can't be a coincidence."

The screaming intensified, the sound of a panicked crowd running from gunfire. Morgan knew that they would be outnumbered if they stayed to fight.

They had to run.

"This way," Nataline said, leading the way out of the garden. "We can get round the back of the church and into the streets beyond. We'll lose them there."

They ducked down into an alleyway, Morgan and Jake at the rear to cover their escape.

A bullet pinged near their heads and a rattle of gunfire peppered their location.

"Keep going," Morgan shouted to Nataline and Ben. "We'll be right behind you."

The two hurried on as Morgan and Jake returned fire until the gunman receded.

Morgan spun around to find Nataline and Ben out of sight, the dogleg streets hiding their location. She and Jake ran onwards and rounded a corner into a suddenly quiet alleyway. People had melted into doorways, standing silently. Even the dogs had stopped barking.

"Something's wrong." Morgan's heart pounded. "Where are they?"

She sprinted to the end of the alley to see Nataline and Father Ben being bundled into a sedan car. Men with automatic weapons stood by the vehicle, muzzles pointed at Morgan and Jake.

"Morgan!" Ben's voice was weak, and she started towards him.

Jake pulled her away as the men by the car opened fire, driving them back into the alley.

As they drove off, Morgan pushed Jake away and fell to her knees, her eyes filling with tears as she realized how much she had failed Ben. They had to get after the men.

Jake's phone rang and he answered it quickly.

"We have a situation, Martin."

He fell silent and his face paled as he turned to Morgan.

"They have Marietti too."

CHAPTER 18

THE STREETS BEGAN TO fill again, busy with people continuing with their own daily drama, the little scene quickly forgotten. Morgan and Jake ducked into a side street, away from prying eyes. The heat was now oppressive, the sounds about them threatening. The knife-edge of India had shifted in just a few minutes.

Jake put Martin on speakerphone.

"Marietti was abducted from the hospital twenty minutes ago," he said, his voice crackling a little over the line. Morgan could hear his concern and she felt an echo of it inside herself. "He was unconscious when they took him, but he has a tracker implant. He insisted on having one inserted a few months back. I wondered why at the time, but clearly he's been worried about something like this." A pause, and then Martin's usual no-nonsense voice came back on. "Oh, don't worry, you two don't have one."

"I'm actually thinking it might be a good idea," Jake said, shaking his head. "So are you tracking him right now?"

"Yes, and they're clearly heading towards Heathrow Airport. Of course, I could notify the police before he's taken out of the country–"

"But to find Ben and Nataline, we need to leave him in play," Morgan interrupted. "We have to assume that they'll be held in the same place by the same people who took the sculpture piece."

Jake kneaded his temples with his fists, his muscles tense with anxiety. "But Marietti is unconscious. The travel might just make his injuries worse. We have to get him back to hospital."

Morgan put her hand on Jake's arm. "You know Marietti. He clearly expected something like this and he kept it quiet, presumably because he didn't want to jeopardize anyone else's safety. From what Ben said about his past with Sister Nataline, he would want us to go after her … and I'm going after Ben, whatever it takes. This is the best lead we have. Please, Jake."

Morgan watched conflict flicker over his features, concern for the man he respected above all others jostling with the desire to follow the mission to the end.

Finally, he nodded. "So be it. Martin, let them leave but keep tabs on that plane and as soon as it's clear where they're heading, get us on a flight. We'll head back to the airport and await your call."

Back at Goa Airport, they found a corner to wait. Morgan curled up on a hard plastic chair and pulled her headscarf around her eyes to block out the light. She could sleep anywhere and while they could do nothing but worry, it seemed better to rest and be ready for the next step. The last thing she saw before she pulled the scarf down was Jake, his jawline taut with tension, his fists clenched on the chair arms, his body braced for action. He had come back from New York a physically stronger man, but he still had his demons. She slipped into sleep.

"Morgan, wake up."

She pulled the scarf from around her eyes, blinking at the harsh light of the airport.

"The plane has landed in Kolkata." Jake held his phone out and she could just make out the sound of tapping.

"There's a plane in the next thirty minutes," Martin's tinny voice said. "The flight will take just a couple of hours.

You'll be there by nightfall. By then, I should know exactly where they've taken Marietti."

And Ben, Morgan thought, conjuring his familiar face. As Jake loved Marietti in his way, so she realized that she loved Ben. After her father had died, murdered in Israel as one of the Remnant, Ben had played the part of mentor and guide.

She had to find him.

"We're on our way," said Jake.

* * *

Each minute seemed like an hour as they traveled east towards Kolkata, formerly known as Calcutta. Jake gazed out the window, lost in thought. He suddenly realized that his fists were tightly clenched and he deliberately relaxed them, exhaling as he tried to release the tension in his body.

He was angry with Marietti for working alone and not telling anyone about his concerns for the sculpture piece. The man was not an island anymore, not when there were ARKANE agents in the field who depended upon him. And yet, Jake knew that his anger was more personal. His own father had been massacred along with the rest of his family in South Africa, and in the last twenty years the greatest impact on his life had been first the military and then ARKANE … and Marietti.

Jake thought back to that night in South Sudan when they had stood on the veranda of one of the local houses listening to the sounds of the African night. The croak of cicadas, the patter of gentle rain and the smell of frangipani trees were suddenly broken by shouts of surprise and then screams of pain as the militia took more lives in an endless civil war. That night he and Marietti had witnessed harsh brutality and yet they were not allowed to intervene. Nowadays, Jake hated politics and it was a relief to work with ARKANE, spanning the borders of country and religion.

Marietti had spoken that night of a greater evil that lurked on the edge of civilization, how they could not hope to defeat man's everyday violence, but that Jake could choose to join the greater fight. This supernatural battle wasn't about one army or one country, it was about light versus darkness.

That night, the bush around them had reeked of blood and death, the stink of hatred and violence. They couldn't stop that evil but since then, Jake had worked with ARKANE to prevent nights like it. Sometimes they failed, but each win was another chink of light. After some missions, he dared hope that someday ARKANE would triumph and banish that which crept in the shadows for the last time. But now this blow at the heart of the organization. Why hadn't Marietti shared his concerns?

"You OK?" Morgan said. She put her hand on his and squeezed gently.

Jake turned to look into her blue eyes, the violet slash in her right eye brighter as the light from the window rested on her face. In that moment, he wanted to take her in his arms and lose himself in her embrace. What was the point of all this striving if in the end, the darkness triumphed?

Perhaps together they could forget the fight and move on.

No, Jake thought. Morgan was just as addicted to this life as he was and they fought for something greater than themselves.

But as he looked at her, a dark sliver of doubt crept into his heart. He wanted to tell her to leave, to forget ARKANE, because one day he might be just as worried about her as he was about Marietti.

There were few people he really loved left in the world.

He couldn't lose her too.

"I could really use a beer," he said and reached up to press the call button. The hostess brought them two cold Kingfishers and Jake took a long swig, banishing his dark thoughts.

"I know you're worried about Ben," he said after a moment. "But they're really after Marietti and what he knows of the sculpture piece."

Morgan sighed. "That's what worries me. Ben doesn't know enough, so why would they even keep him alive? I shouldn't have involved him in this, but he was so eager to help."

"He loves you," Jake said softly. "He'd help you with anything, you know that."

"True, but I think he's forgotten how old he really is." Morgan smiled. "He likes to pretend he's an agent like us."

Jake laughed. "I hope I'm as sprightly as he is when I'm his age." He pulled out his phone and tapped it to bring up the information that Martin had sent. "We might as well check out Kolkata before we land."

He scrolled through the images, a juxtaposition of the extravagant Victoria Memorial, a hangover from the British Raj, and the slums of grey, high-density dwellings where millions eked out a living within the pulse of the city.

Morgan leaned over to see the images more clearly. "I think people in the West associate Calcutta with Mother Teresa, but it seems quite a different place these days as a hub of technology and culture."

Jake pulled up pictures of India's oldest port, situated on the banks of the Hooghly River.

"The capital of West Bengal, the third biggest city in India behind Mumbai and Delhi. How the hell are we going to find Marietti here?"

As the announcement came over the tannoy that the plane was descending, Jake's phone vibrated and he pulled it out to find a text from Martin. "The tracker has stopped moving."

He clicked the link and a map opened up, zooming in to the detail of the city.

"That's Kalighat." he said. "A temple to the goddess Kali."

"She's an aspect of the goddess Durga," Morgan whispered. "A black goddess, representing the forces of time and destruction. She's usually portrayed with a garland of human heads and she holds a freshly decapitated one. Her hands are bloody from sacrifice and her tongue is red with the blood of the demon Raktabija whose blood she spilled and drank."

"Oh, great," Jake said, and took a final swig of his beer. "This should be fun."

They landed as night fell and jumped in a taxi from the airport. Marietti's tracker had gone dark soon after it had stopped moving, so they could only hope he was still being held at the Kali temple.

"I'm sure he's been taken underground or something. There's nothing to worry about." Morgan's voice was confident, but Jake could hear her concern. He reached for her hand and she let it rest in his.

"Definitely," he replied. "That's the only explanation."

They drove through the city and arrived at the Kalighat temple on the bank of the Tolly canal, which ran down from the Hooghly River further north.

"Some say that the name Calcutta stems from the word Kalighat," Morgan said, as they looked up at the imposing structure. "The river once ran past here but over time it moved north."

The temple was attractive from the outside, with cream domes and archways highlighted in terracotta paint. It was busy with pilgrims come to pay respect to the goddess. Many Indians treated the goddess Kali as a mother figure, bringing her the problems of domestic life and asking for prosperity. A woman bustled past, a wreath of marigolds in her hand, and Morgan and Jake followed her inside the temple through a dark corridor towards an open courtyard.

The sound of bleating made them stop and turn. A goat

stood tethered in front of a sacrificial altar, rust red with faded bloodstains. A priest lifted his scimitar and with one quick stroke, he sliced the head from the goat. Fresh blood spurted out onto the altar as the lifeless corpse slumped to the ground, still twitching. Jake understood that animal sacrifice was still common across the world, and if he was honest, this manner of death was more humane than many Western abattoirs. But it still made him shiver a little as worshippers dipped cloth into the blood as a blessing.

They walked on towards the idol, a portrayal of the goddess at the heart of the temple. They moved with the crowd of pilgrims, the smell of bodies and incense and smoke creating a heady atmosphere, until they finally emerged in front of Kali herself. The sound of whispered prayers filled the chamber as pilgrims paraded past the statue of the goddess. It was unusual, with three eyes on black skin and a golden protruding tongue. In two hands she held a golden severed head and a sword while the other two hands were curled into the *mudra* prayer position.

"There's no way Marietti is here," Jake whispered. "Look at this crowd. It's just another temple full of the faithful."

"But the tracker went dead here," Morgan said as they exited the chamber. "So where else could they have gone?"

CHAPTER 19

MARIETTI HEARD CHANTING AS he regained consciousness, a repetition of a mantra that vibrated through him. The smell of incense lay heavy in the air and underneath it, the metallic tang of blood. He was bound upright against a pillar of some kind, ropes holding him tight.

He opened his eyes.

He was in an ancient temple with a low ceiling and walls painted with aspects of the divine. Before him, next to a bloodstained altar, was a huge statue of Kali, the black goddess of time and change, creation and destruction. At the feet of the goddess, a dreadlocked sadhu sat cross-legged, his body covered in ash, his dark eyes dilated as he sipped from a human skull. His eyes were fixed at some point beyond the physical realm. Rows of devotees knelt facing their goddess and their bodies swayed as they chanted a hymn of death and blood.

A man was bound to the pillar on his right. His old face was turned away, but Marietti recognized Father Ben Costanza. What was he doing there?

"Elias." A soft voice spoke to his left. A voice he hadn't heard for many years.

Marietti turned his head.

Nataline was bound to the pillar next to him, her face still beautiful, her eyes bright even though they looked hollow in the flickering candlelight.

A sudden realization stabbed through him. The sculpture. The bomb. It was all his fault.

"I'm so sorry," he whispered, his voice cracking with emotion. "I didn't mean–"

"Young love, it's so sweet." A woman stepped out of the shadows behind them. She untied Nataline, releasing the nun from the bonds. "There, go to him."

Nataline rushed to Marietti, her soft lips on his after so long. He closed his eyes and the years fell away. They were back on the beach in Goa, laughing together in the blue waters of the Arabian Sea – before he had chosen another path. Nataline's fingers found his and she began to work on the knots that held him.

The woman pulled her away. "That's enough."

Two bodyguards stepped forward from the shadows and forced Nataline to her knees in front of the altar, their heavy hands on her shoulders. Marietti wanted to shout for them to stop, to take him instead, but he held his tongue. He needed more time to figure out what was going on.

The woman came to stand close to Marietti and looked up into his dark eyes.

"You think you're untouchable, but I was the one who took the sculpture piece from your vault."

"Just one piece," Marietti whispered, a smile playing about his lips. "There is no worth in that and you know it. You don't have all the pieces or I wouldn't be here."

The woman smiled, but he saw the flash of anger in her eyes.

"Do you know of Kali Yuga?" she asked.

Marietti frowned. "The age of vice, or the age of the demon Kali. Supposedly the last of four stages the world goes through as part of the cycle of time."

"When the people are far from the gods and human civilization degenerates," the woman continued. "Then the end will come and Lord Shiva will judge us and the end of time will be upon us."

Marietti raised an eyebrow. "That is not my faith."

"You Christians have a similar apocalyptic vision in the tribulation, a time of great trouble before the end times. So we are not so different. But I believe we can hold this time back by offering a great sacrifice that will make the gods see we are still faithful." She spun around, indicating the devotees chanting behind her. "We are the faithful." She turned back to Marietti. "But I need that sculpture intact. I need the Brahmastra. Tell me where the other pieces are or ..."

She nodded towards Nataline, her eyes narrowing.

Marietti stared back at her, his face implacable. But inside, he was screaming. Not Nataline, please God. It was only one life against the possibility of mass slaughter, but it was her life and he had sworn to keep her from trouble. He wanted Nataline to die an old woman in the golden light of Goa after a life of service that made her happy. The thought of her there had kept him at peace for many years, and now she was threatened because of him.

The woman spun to the altar and picked up a kukri, the sharp blade reflecting the light of the candles lit around the temple. A low hiss came from the devotees and their chanting doubled in intensity, their eyes fixed on the blade. Marietti could sense their excitement and bile rose in his throat at what she threatened.

The bodyguards pushed Nataline forward onto the altar, pulling her long hair away from her neck to expose the paler skin there. Skin he had kissed long ago.

"The goddess demands her sacrifice," the woman said. "Now, where are they?"

Marietti hung his head, eyes closed as he prayed for a way out of this, for some sign of what he should do.

"Elias." He looked up into Nataline's eyes as she lay on the altar. He saw love and forgiveness in the depths, and an unshakeable faith that made his own a poor reflection. "Don't let her win."

At her words, the woman turned.

"Hold out her hand."

The bodyguards stretched out Nataline's arm as she struggled against them. The woman raised the kukri and with one swift stroke, she severed Nataline's hand.

It fell to the floor, a pale offering in a growing pool of blood.

One of the devotees cried out as if in ecstasy. Nataline paled, her eyes fixed on the severed limb as her lips moved in prayer. Marietti knew the shock would prevent pain for only a second and she would lose a lot of blood quickly. Desperation rose within him.

The woman went to the sadhu and picked up his skull bowl. She held it to the end of the spurting wrist until it filled with blood. She handed it back to her guru and he drank deep, crimson staining his lips.

Marietti retched, coughing as tears ran down his cheeks.

"The next blow will be her head." The woman's voice was a sick caress, an offering from the dark and Marietti felt like he was on the edge of the abyss. The devil's choice to save a woman he loved and let the rest of the world be damned.

"Even though I walk through the valley of the shadow of death, I fear no evil, for You are with me." Nataline's voice was strong in the temple, loud enough to echo around the walls above the heads of the chanting devotees. Marietti let the words of Psalm 23 wash over him and he was shamed by Nataline's faith.

The woman's face filled with anger and her fingers tightened on the handle of the kukri.

"I will dwell in the house of the Lord forever."

Marietti spoke the final words along with Nataline, their voices joined in prayer.

"So be it," the woman said, and raised the blade above her head, adjusting her position for the final blow.

The bodyguards held Nataline down and one pulled her hair tight so her neck was at the right angle. Marietti wanted to turn away but he had to witness it. He had to see the death he had caused.

The blade flashed down and in one clean stroke, Nataline's head was severed from her body. Blood ran down the altar as a collective gasp rose from the devotees.

Marietti slumped in his bonds, all strength leaving his body as he wept for Nataline, the love he had lost once again, this time forever. Her blood was on his soul, another stain to add to his many sins.

The woman bent to the corpse and dipped her fingers in the pool of blood.

She reached up and forced her bloody fingers into Marietti's mouth. The salt tang made him retch once more.

"Taste it," the woman said. "You could have saved her."

"She gave her life to stop you finding that final piece," Marietti spat. "Nataline believed in God and she is with Him now."

"Then we may as well send another to your God, and my goddess can drink her fill today."

The bodyguards untied Father Ben from the pillar and thrust him forward onto his knees at the altar. He stared down at Nataline's body as her blood soaked into his clothes. He clutched a hand over his mouth and his eyes filled with tears.

"One more chance," the woman said, her eyes fixed on Marietti.

CHAPTER 20

MORGAN AND JAKE MOVED away from the inner sanctum and stood watching the faithful as they crowded in to see the goddess. What were they missing?

"At some rural places in India, it's reported that human sacrifice is still carried out to honor the goddess Kali," Morgan said. "The severed hands and heads are left in exchange for her blessing. Maybe there are some here who still believe in such extremes?"

"Worth a try," Jake said. "Maybe if Martin can get information on unusual deaths in the city, especially those with missing hands or decapitations, we might be able to narrow down the area to search."

He started to text on his phone, and Morgan continued to scan the crowd. Then a man walked past, looking around furtively. He was thin and he limped, his clothes were ragged and threadbare, and one of his hands was missing.

"Look, Jake. Perhaps he knows something."

Jake nodded and silently they slipped into the crowd after him.

The man stopped at the altar to dip his handkerchief in the blood that still dripped from the goat's body, then he walked to the corner of the compound. He suddenly looked around, away from the crowd, and Jake and Morgan could no longer remain unseen. Jake quickly walked up to the man, his tall physique overshadowing the smaller figure.

"Where are you going?" Jake demanded. "Is there another part of the temple?"

"Please, sir, I don't know of what you speak." The man's English was stumbling but his eyes betrayed a greater knowledge.

Morgan pulled out a wad of rupees, enough to keep the man's family for several months. She hoped it was enough.

"We just want to pay our respects to the goddess," she said. "Will you take us?" The man reached out a shaking hand for the money but Morgan held it back. She handed him a few notes as a promise. "The rest when we're inside."

The man nodded. "Then you must approach with care or the goddess will be displeased. Come, you must prepare."

He dabbed his still-bloody handkerchief on his own fore-head and then indicated that they should lean towards him. He pressed the blood against their heads in turn, leaving a scarlet mark.

Morgan could smell the metallic tang of the goat's blood and it sickened her in a way. But another part of her, the ancient side that descended from Jews who worshipped in the temple at Jerusalem, understood the need to sacrifice to a deity.

For what offering was more potent than blood?

The man led them away from the crowded temple and through a labyrinth of corridors, each one angling off the next in a dizzying array of twists and turns. Morgan soon lost her bearings. The walls shifted from the cream and terracotta of the main temple to plain stone as the cor-ridors narrowed and at some point they crossed from the nineteenth-century temple to somewhere far older.

Suddenly they heard voices ahead. The man's steps slowed.

"It is usually quiet here," he said with a frown.

Hope rose inside Morgan at his words.

Jake indicated that the man should go ahead and they walked a few paces behind him, hiding in the shadows of the corridor as he approached a huge ceremonial door. It was decorated with severed heads, each with a different expression of anguish, but all dripped with blood.

The man approached the two guards on the door and they had a brief conversation. Then the man turned away and walked back down the corridor.

"We cannot enter the inner temple today," he said. "There is a special sacrifice for the goddess. I will come back tomorrow."

Morgan handed over the rest of the rupees and the man walked away down the corridor.

As his footsteps faded, she felt the familiar rise of adrenalin in anticipation of a fight. These people had taken Marietti, Ben and Sister Nataline. She and Jake were going through that door. The question was whether these men would stop them.

They both pulled their weapons.

There was no need for words between them and Morgan appreciated that. She trusted Jake, and she could see the excitement in his eyes.

He indicated that he would go left and she could take the one on the right.

They walked out of the tunnel with confident steps.

The guards on the door turned and reached for their weapons.

Morgan and Jake aimed and fired in unison, body shots to bring the men down. The guards fell back against the wall, clutching at their chests. Jake stepped closer and finished them both off.

The goddess had her sacrifice for today.

Together they pushed open the huge double doors. Inside was an empty anteroom, but they could hear chanting through a great arch ahead. The low sound vibrated through Morgan's chest, the repetition of sacred sound a mantra to the goddess.

They continued on, weapons outstretched before them, and walked into the inner sanctum.

A crowd of devotees swayed in prayer, some with hands raised as they chanted. A magnificent statue of Kali towered above them in her Destroyer aspect, her body made of polished black basalt. In her outstretched hands she held a bloody sword and a newly severed head, still dripping crimson drops onto the altar below.

Morgan gasped.

The head was Sister Nataline's.

"No," she whispered and desperation filled her, all caution forgotten in her concern for Ben. She pushed through the crowd. Jake followed close behind until he grabbed her, right on the edge of the altar area, holding her back as they witnessed the tableau before them.

Marietti stood bound to a pillar, his face ragged with sorrow.

The decapitated body of Sister Nataline lay at his feet, one hand cut off as well as her head. A woman stood with a kukri in her hands and behind her sat a dreadlocked sadhu painted with ash.

A bodyguard shoved another bound figure forward.

Father Ben fell to his knees before the altar. He moaned as he saw Sister Nataline and his dusty habit darkened as it soaked in her blood.

"One more chance," the woman said, her eyes fixed on Marietti.

"I'm sorry, Ben," Marietti whispered. "You know I can't. There are too many lives at stake."

The woman raised the kukri above her head.

"No!" Morgan shouted.

She tore out of Jake's grasp and scrambled onto the altar stage. Jake leapt up behind her, gun out. Bodyguards surrounded them, weapons pointed at the intruders.

The woman stopped, her blade hovering above Ben's neck.

"I have the piece you want," Morgan said. She pulled the

wrapped sculpture piece from her bag. "Let them go."

"I'd do as she says." Jake stood behind Morgan, his gun pointing straight at the woman's head.

The woman lowered her blade and a slow smile spread across her lips.

"You two beat me to the Taj Mahal. I heard about you from your guide. Of course, he's with the goddess now." She stepped forward. "Do you seriously think that if you shoot me you'll get out of here with your friends alive?"

Jake shrugged. "I'm thinking that you want out of here as well, so I'll take my chances." He kept his gun trained on her as the woman stepped forward to examine what Morgan held.

"Is that the piece from the crypt?"

Morgan nodded. "Yes, and you can have it in exchange for these two men."

"Two men for the final *two* pieces." She raised the kukri over Ben's neck again. "Or the goddess gets her sacrifice."

Father Ben looked up at Morgan, his eyes pleading with her. She saw that he would go to his God in order to save her, but she wasn't ready to give up yet.

"You'll have your two pieces."

Marietti raised his head at her confident tone. His bloody lips were cracked and broken but he managed to speak, his voice hoarse.

"She doesn't know where the final piece is. Only I do."

Morgan's heart thumped as she stood there. Why would Marietti try to stop her? Why did he court death this way? Was the sculpture truly so powerful that he would die before he allowed the piece to be found?

Well, she would not allow it. She would take Ben home and Marietti too.

"I can find it," she said.

The woman narrowed her eyes. "How are you so sure?"

Morgan took a deep breath. She wasn't sure, but something solidified in her mind even as she faced their enemy. The kaleidoscope of what they knew of Marietti's life, the pictures in his photo album and what Jake had said about the destruction in Africa all coalesced into one idea. Marietti had witnessed mass murder before, and if he believed the piece of the sculpture could create such death, then perhaps he would hide it in the place he still had nightmares about.

"He will never tell you where it is," Morgan said. "You can kill us all and he will never tell and you won't complete the sculpture. But he can't hide the footprints of the past. Give me forty-eight hours and I will find the final piece."

The woman lowered the kukri and turned to the seated sadhu. His ash-rimmed eyes looked at Morgan as she stood unflinching before him. She felt him rake her soul and something inside her curled away at his intrusion.

Finally, the sadhu nodded.

"So be it," the woman said. She walked towards Morgan and Jake, her hips swinging in a sinuous manner. She was beautiful, sensual, even covered in blood. "I'll take this as part payment." She reached for the package and Morgan relinquished it into her grasp. "If you can indeed find the last piece within forty-eight hours, then these two will be released. If not …"

She turned and nodded to her bodyguards. They dragged Ben and Marietti away as the men sagged, defeated, in their bonds. Morgan could only hope that they would be able to hang on for just a little longer.

"I want them unharmed," she said.

"Of course." The woman gave a little bow. She turned and spoke to another of the bodyguards. She took his phone, tapped into it for a second and then handed it to Morgan. "Take this. I'll text the location for you to bring the piece … and I'll send a photo of their heads if you're not on time."

She turned and swept out of the temple.

The sadhu rose to his feet, his eyes empty, like a shadow

who lived in the world but was not of it. His footsteps were silent as he walked behind her.

The crowd of devotees melted back into the corridors beyond and within minutes, the temple was empty. The only evidence left was the head of Sister Nataline hanging on the outstretched hand of the goddess Kali, still dripping blood onto the altar.

Morgan fell to her knees, exhaustion suddenly overwhelming her. She felt dizzy and weak. Sister Nataline's head seemed to stare right at her, an accusation of her failure. If only they had arrived earlier. If only …

Jake knelt next to her and pulled her against him. She could hear his heart beating and she rested her head against his chest.

"What were you thinking?" he whispered. "We could have tried to take them."

"You saw how many there were." She looked up at him. "We wouldn't have stood a chance. At least this way we're still alive to fight another day."

"But how will we find the final piece?" Jake's corkscrew scar crinkled at the question, his brown eyes quizzical. "Marietti has never told anyone where it is and it seems that he would die to protect it."

"And let others die for him, Jake. What if it had been you here instead of Sister Nataline?"

He shook his head. "I'm not sure. I thought I knew him …"

"Well, I'm not willing to stand by and let someone I love die." Tears welled and ran down her cheeks. "Marietti may be able to give up, but I won't. Ben didn't ask to be part of this and once again I've dragged him into a mission and put him in danger." She stood and wrapped her arms around herself as the cold night seeped in through the temple walls. "I'm livid with Marietti. How dare he?"

Jake looked up at the severed head of Sister Nataline. "I

don't think he knows how to love anymore." He shook his head. "Perhaps he never did. He only sees the bigger picture, the potential for mass slaughter if the sculpture is used as some kind of weapon."

"You and I have faced the darkness before," Morgan said, "and I come from a different faith anyway. The Talmud says that 'whoever saves a life, it is as if he saved an entire world.'" She pointed up at the severed head. "We failed Sister Nataline, but I will not fail Ben."

Jake nodded. "I'm with you. I still want to get Marietti back, even if you're only gonna kill him yourself." He smiled softly. "Right, we have forty-eight hours. Where are we going?"

CHAPTER 21

Kigali, Rwanda, Africa. 11.48am

"IT'S BEEN A LONG time since I was here," Jake said, as they emerged from the airport in Kigali. It was just as hot and dusty and busy as Kolkata had been, with taxi drivers shouting for custom and people embracing in tears. He hailed one of the local cabs and they got in. "I had only just started in the military in 1994 and the killing here had already escalated before the world really took notice. We came as peacekeepers to help with the aftermath. I still have nightmares about that time."

"But Marietti was here during the worst of it, wasn't he?" Morgan said, as they drove along the highway out of the airport and headed north. "There was a picture in his photo album in front of a mass grave. He wanted to remember how much it affected him and I think it's why he can't see one death as important anymore. He'll do anything to prevent murder on such a scale again."

"That's why you think he buried the piece here?" Jake said. "But how can you be so sure?"

"I'm not, but I'm staking Ben's life on it. And Marietti's, of course, although I doubt he'll appreciate the effort." Morgan grimaced, imagining the Director's wrath even if they did get him out of the clutches of Kali.

"He's a tough old man," Jake said. "I don't think you or I know how much he has done under the auspices of

ARKANE, or of the horrors he has faced to keep people safe. I know you're angry with him, Morgan, but we'll get through this somehow." He looked out the window. "At least I hope we will."

Morgan pulled out a map marked with five black crosses.

"These are the closest memorials to the city," she said as she showed Jake the proposed route between them. "Marietti was never here very long when he came back to visit, so I'm assuming that the picture we saw is from one of these rather than the others around the country."

They drove through the dirt of the city out to a rural area where rows of green palm trees divided small plots of land. A group of smiling children ran down the road after the car, their white teeth flashing in the sun.

It was a fertile place, rejuvenated in the last ten years as Rwanda invested in crop intensification. Farmers here now made enough to export as well as feed their families. Deep green tea plantations dotted the hills and there were gorillas in the high forests near the border with Congo and Uganda. It was a beautiful country and Morgan wished they could be here under other circumstances. After all, Jake was African and he knew this continent. The knife-edge of glorious life and beauty and intense experience, and the shadows too. India had the same sense of being closer to real life, not separated from it by years of uptight repression as she sometimes felt in England.

They soon pulled up at the first memorial but without even getting out the car, Morgan knew it wasn't the right one. The topography was all wrong. She sighed.

Jake looked at his watch. "We still have time. Let's go on to the next one."

They were hot and tired when they finally arrived at the Murambi Genocide Memorial, a school that had been the site of a massacre during the conflict, and the fourth on Morgan's list. It was on a hill overlooking fields of green and hills beyond. Chickens scratched in the ground nearby, but the peace and normality hid a troubled past.

"This is it," Morgan said as they got out the car. "It has to be."

A local guide came to greet them, her gentle smile welcoming even as her eyes held great sorrow. She led Morgan and Jake into the compound.

"Tutsis sheltered here to try and escape the violence, but in fact they were herded into such places to make it easier to kill them in larger groups. It's estimated that 45,000 people were murdered here in just a few days. Their bodies were buried in pits and a volleyball court built over the mass grave to hide the evidence."

Her stark words did nothing to hide the horror of what had happened here. The blood of innocents soaked into the earth beneath their feet and Morgan understood, for Israel was the same. Years of conflict, so much blood spilled, and still, no resolution.

The guide led them towards a series of brick huts, her steps heavy. She pushed open the first door.

"Please," she said, nodding inside.

Morgan walked in first and it took a moment for her eyes to adjust to the darkness.

Then she saw them.

Mummified bodies lay on wooden racks, white from the lime they had been exhumed from, the bodies squashed almost flat from the way they had been stacked in death. Some wore ragged clothes, one had a rosary around its neck. One figure had tufts of hair and another lay with its mouth open, frozen in a final scream. Many had limbs missing and cracked skulls, killed with machetes and farm implements. On another rack, skulls piled high, some cracked and broken.

"Most of the dead from the massacre here were given a dignified burial," the guide said quietly. "But these corpses are displayed openly to stop denial of the genocide."

Morgan nodded, thinking of those who denied the millions of Jewish dead in the Second World War.

"I understand that," she whispered. "The dead are past suffering, but unless we are confronted with the results of such action, how are people to learn from what happened here."

The guide walked to the door.

"Come to the next room. It has the younger children aged three to six years old."

Jake had been quiet but now he visibly paled. Morgan remembered how he had reacted in the crypt of Palermo at the sight of the mummified children. She wanted to reach for his hand to let him know she understood, but he crossed his arms, tucking his hands underneath his armpits, as if he were chilled to the bone.

"I'm going to wait outside," he said, his voice cracking a little. "Call if you need me."

He walked outside and Morgan let him go.

But she needed to see, and bear witness to the atrocity.

In the children's room there were many more bodies, tiny figures curled in death. A wreath of fresh flowers had been left amongst them, the heavy scent of lilies hanging in the air. Morgan wanted to cry, but these were not her people to mourn. A human life was just the flash of a firefly in the night and she could only try to help keep the light alive.

"Why did it happen?" she asked, wanting the woman to tell her story.

The guide took a deep breath. "On April 6, 1994, a suspicious plane crash killed the president, a Hutu, the majority tribe of Rwanda. The Hutus turned on the Tutsi minority in retribution and it's thought that up to a million people were killed in the months following. Neighbors turned against each other and there was widespread rape and maiming as well as murder. Families were torn apart if there had been intermarriage. It was indeed a dark time and it has taken us many years to recover. Of course, we will not forget." She looked down at the bodies. "Some of my own family were taken." Then she looked up, her eyes blazing. "They called us cockroaches. They saw us as less than human, although days before, we were neighbors."

Her words shocked Morgan because it was the same word that Hitler had used for Jews, the same word used even now against migrants and refugees, the same word used to dehumanize the Other.

"I'm so sorry," she said, putting her hand out to the woman and touching her sleeve. She wondered how the guide could stand seeing this every day, but then if everyone moved on, there would be no one left to remember.

Morgan looked around at the bodies, the number who lay dead here. If the statue was put together again, could the Brahmastra weapon really do as much damage as humans had here? Or was Marietti just haunted by a past he couldn't change? Was it all just an exaggerated myth?

Morgan didn't know, but she was certain that she would not let Ben be one of the dead.

"Are there any foreign tributes here?" she asked the guide, turning away from the skeletal remains. "Anything from overseas aid organizations?"

"There is a memorial area," the guide said. "Come. It's through here."

They walked along the corridor into a simple room. The walls were painted a stark white and a row of benches faced a memorial sculpture. It portrayed a family huddled together in polished black stone, their faces upturned to heaven. Two bunches of colorful flowers rested against the plaque on the wall next to it, and a low table in the corner held an open Visitors Book.

"People of all faiths come here to pray," the guide said. "Many of the murdered were Christian, some were Muslim, some of the tribal faith, so this room is where all can come to remember. It was paid for by an anonymous donor."

Morgan looked around the room. There was nowhere immediately obvious where Marietti might have hidden a piece of the sculpture, but the guide's mention of an anonymous donor gave her hope.

"Do you mind if I sit here for a moment?" she asked.

The guide nodded. "Of course, I'll leave you and wait with your friend outside."

She left the room and Morgan sat down for a moment as she absorbed the feeling of the place.

It was desolate, the walls saturated with the collected grief of half a nation. She had felt this before in the chambers at Auschwitz and in the killing fields of Cambodia, and she understood Marietti's reasons for caring so much.

Martin Klein had sent as much as he could find on Marietti's many trips to Africa over the years. The Director had visited Kigali on the anniversary of the massacre most years, but of course, there were many memorials, many other places where he could have left the sculpture piece.

If it was even in Rwanda at all.

It has to be. Because if it isn't …

She stood, walked over to the table and flipped through the Visitors Book. It was sparse and the entries grew further apart as the years went on. Many of the comments were from foreigners, dark tourists drawn to places like this. Proximity to death made the sweetness and brevity of life more prominent, and perhaps that was why she and Jake would struggle to ever leave ARKANE.

The Visitors Book was no use so she walked over to the plaque next to the memorial. It was a carved piece of stone etched with the dates of the massacre and the number of lives lost in this area.

But then she noticed something.

The stone seemed to float away from the wall. Morgan pressed her cheek against the plaster to try and see behind it.

Her heart beat faster. She didn't want to do anything to desecrate this memorial place, but she had to know if there was something here.

She ran her fingers around the edge and then pulled the plaque towards her slightly to test its movement. It was more slender than she had expected and she was able to lift it up easily. It came away in her hands and she placed it carefully on the floor.

Behind it was a safe with a combination lock.

Morgan's heart fell. They didn't have much time.

She called Martin and he answered on the first ring.

"Morgan, what's going on? Have you found something?"

She switched on the video function on her phone and aimed it at the safe.

"We're at one of the genocide memorial sites and I found this safe but it's a combination lock. I don't even know if Marietti left it here but I need to get inside."

"Zoom the camera closer," Martin said.

Morgan walked forward until the lock filled the entire screen.

"That model is commonly used in Italy and I know Marietti has a version for his personal office safe. There is a chance that he left it here. Let's have a look at possible number combinations." The sound of tapping came from the phone as Martin probed the ARKANE database. "I can look at Marietti's passwords to see if any of those might give us a clue."

Morgan waited in the silence of the room.

"OK," Martin said, a moment later. "Here's something. Try 160867. That's the date Marietti joined the Vatican."

Morgan typed the numbers in.

There was a second of silence then a loud beep.

"That's no good," she said. "And we have to hurry."

Suddenly footsteps echoed down the hallway and the door creaked as it opened.

CHAPTER 22

"TRY 521221," JAKE SAID as he walked into the room. His face was calm again, his darkness lifted and Morgan sighed with relief to see him and not the guide or another Rwandan official.

She typed the code into the keypad.

A moment later, the lock clicked and the door popped ajar.

"What does that stand for?" she asked.

"Marietti's favorite Bible quote. Romans, the fifty-second book of the Catholic Bible, chapter 12 verse 21."

Morgan tilted her head to one side as she recalled the words.

"Do not be overcome by evil, but overcome evil with good."

Jake grinned. "Show-off. Bet you didn't know that he has it tattooed on him as well."

Morgan raised an eyebrow. "Seriously?"

Jake nodded. "But if I told you where, I'd have to kill you." He reached for the door of the safe. "Now, let's see what's inside."

He pulled the door fully open to reveal a pile of paper that reached almost to the top. Morgan pulled off the first sheet.

"It's a list of names." She scanned the page. "The names of the dead. It makes sense to have them here behind the Memorial."

She thought of the Holocaust memorials around the world. In the ghetto of Prague, the names of the dead were written on the walls and a voice read them out all hours of the day. In Jerusalem at Yad Vashem, the names were read by candlelight. Here they were kept hidden, but it didn't make them any less real.

Jake leaned forward and lifted the pile of paper out. "There's something behind."

Morgan reached in and pulled out a package wrapped in layers of plastic. It was rectangular, the right size for the missing part of the sculpture base. She tugged open the edge of the plastic to reveal the dull bronze sheen of the final piece.

A huge weight lifted as she realized that Ben would be OK, even though she could see by Jake's face that he considered it a mixed blessing.

"We've got it, Martin," she said.

"Thank goodness," Martin replied over the phone line. "Now you can get Marietti and Father Ben back. Speak soon."

The phone line went dead.

"But what will happen when the statue is put together again?" Jake whispered.

They put the papers back into the safe and closed the door, then rehung the plaque in its original position. It was as if they hadn't even been there, but Morgan knew that she would never forget this place. Her anger at Marietti had dissipated in the face of the past atrocity and if he was worried about this scale of possible death in India, then they still had a fight ahead of them.

Morgan stopped to say goodbye to the guide on the way out and then they walked back to the taxi together, the piece of the sculpture safe in Morgan's backpack.

As they sped back to Kigali, she texted the woman from the Kali temple with a photo of the sculpture piece.

A few minutes later, she received a text in return.

Bring it to Mumbai for the exchange. 12 o'clock tomorrow at the Gateway of India.

Then Morgan texted Martin with an idea. There was a way that they could keep the piece out of Asha's hands and still get Marietti and Ben back. She only hoped it would work.

Mumbai, India. 11.52am

Morgan and Jake stood under the great arch of the Gateway of India, built in the British era to commemorate the visit of King George V and Queen Mary when they visited in 1911. Jake paced up and down, looking at his watch every few seconds but Morgan stood still and leaned against the stone, concentrating on breathing and waiting.

The Gateway perched on the edge of the harbor looking out towards the Arabian Sea. Some would have torn down any symbol of the British Raj but the triumphal arch had symbolic resonance. The final British troops had left through it after India gained independence in 1948 and it was now a symbol of the death of an Empire.

The water was choppy as the wind whipped the waves into peaks. High above, the clouds darkened, heavy with a hint of rain. Tourists thronged the wide courtyard, snapping photos while street vendors hustled with cheap souvenirs. The smell of frying *vada-pav* filled the air and Morgan found her stomach rumbling at the thought of the spicy potato patties served with green chutney. The cry of gulls pierced the air as they wheeled above the harbor diving for scraps, and then a horn blared a deep sonorous note as a ferry docked from the island of Elephanta.

This busy junction had been chosen for its visibility and

it gave Morgan hope that she would see Ben and Marietti again soon. Her backpack was heavy on her shoulders, doubly so because it now contained two bronze sculpture pieces. She had sent Martin the dimensions and photos of the final piece and he had contacted a sculptor in Mumbai who had produced the copy as they had flown back. It really was possible to get anything in India.

The sculptor had delivered it to them this morning, the only difference being that the inscription was not complete. And of course, the radioactive signature would be different. But Morgan carried it next to the original piece with the hope that the fake would pass an initial test, and she was counting on a quick exchange.

She looked at her watch, anxious as the minutes ticked by. They should be here soon.

At exactly twelve o'clock, a limousine pulled up alongside the central archway and two huge bodyguards got out the car. One of the tinted windows wound down with a whirr.

The woman from the temple sat inside, perfectly made up and dressed in an expensive silk sari, her dark hair lacquered. She was the very model of a Mumbai socialite but Morgan knew the reality behind that charming smile.

She beckoned from the window. Morgan walked forward and pulled the fake package, wrapped in brown paper, from her pack.

"Give it to me," the woman said, her bright eyes fixed on the wrapped piece.

"Where are Ben and Marietti?" Morgan demanded.

"Show me the sculpture piece and I'll show you your friends."

Morgan peeled open the edge of the package, enough to reveal half of the bronze base. Her heart beat faster as the woman's eyes narrowed a little.

"It truly is the final piece," the woman whispered. "Oh, you have excelled yourself."

She nodded to the bodyguards and one of them went to the back of the car and opened the trunk. He hauled Ben and Marietti out and they crumpled to the ground, blinking in the daylight. The bodyguard stood over the two men, his hand on his belt to indicate a hidden weapon. Tourists around them ignored the exchange. Just another human drama in a city of millions.

The woman held out her hand. "I keep my word. Give me the package, take your friends and leave India."

Morgan's eyes darted to Ben as he kneeled on the dusty ground. His eyes were pale and unfocused and his hands shook a little. Marietti's broad shoulders slumped and his face was still crusted with blood. They only needed a few minutes to get away.

She handed over the fake package.

The woman barked an order. The bodyguard walked away from the two men, got back in the vehicle and they began to pull out into the traffic.

Morgan and Jake rushed to Ben and Marietti. Morgan threw her arms around Ben and kissed his cheek.

"It's alright, Morgan," he whispered. "I'm OK."

Jake helped Marietti to his feet and the Director stood on shaky legs. But he straightened his back and towered above them, casting a shadow in the midday sun.

He looked down at Morgan, his dark eyes piercing like an Old Testament prophet. He shook his head. "You don't know what you've done."

"Wait," Jake said. "We need to get away from here and then I'll explain–"

His words were cut off by a squeal of brakes.

Doors slamming.

The sound of boots on tarmac.

Morgan spun around to see the bodyguards running from the halted limousine, faces like thunder, hands on their weapons.

There was no time.

She sprinted into the crowd, away from her friends, the backpack with the final piece heavy on her shoulders. If she could just lose them in the busy downtown Mumbai streets …

Angry shouts came from behind her, but no gunshots. They couldn't risk it in such a heavily populated area.

She darted down an alleyway, winding in between shops and insistent vendors, throngs of tourists and colorful merchandise that flashed past as she ran.

Suddenly she was hit from behind, a massive weight bearing her to the ground. The wind was knocked out of her and she gasped for breath.

A fist drove into her side and she retched with pain.

"Stay down," a rough voice whispered. "You're lucky that's not a bullet."

The man pulled the backpack from her and strode off.

People around bent to help Morgan up, chattering in Hindi and pointing after her assailant. But it was too late. She had lost the final piece.

Morgan hung her head as desolation spread through her. Somehow she had believed that they could keep the pieces apart, but now the statue could be put back together. Could it really be used as a weapon?

She limped back to the Gateway.

Jake ran to meet her. "I'm sorry," he said. "I lost you in the crowd. But we'll get it back, I promise."

Together they walked to Ben and Marietti, who sat on a bench near the Gateway as tourists milled around them.

Marietti looked up on their approach. His eyes narrowed as he noticed the backpack was missing. "So they really have it now?"

Morgan nodded.

"Jake, get me away from here." Marietti's voice was cold and Morgan stung with the force of his rejection.

"Wait," Ben said. He reached out and put his hand on Marietti's shirtsleeve, still stained with the blood of Sister Nataline. "There is something that might help. While we were held in the temple, I remembered an ancient story. The Nine Unknown Men swore to protect the most dangerous knowledge of ancient India. It is said that one of their books has the power to stop the greatest weapon, even the Brahmastra."

Hope welled inside Morgan at Ben's words but Marietti laughed, a bark of ridicule. "The books of the Nine Unknown have been hidden for centuries. There's no way we could find even one of them, let alone the right one, in time."

"But it's worth a try," Jake said. "We have nothing left to lose at this point. And…" He held up his phone. "I took a picture of the car. We can trace the number plate and find out who this woman is. Perhaps we can stop her in the old-fashioned way." He looked at Marietti.

The Director's face softened and then he put his hand up to his head as he swayed on his feet. Jake grabbed him around the waist. "But first, we need to get you inside."

The four of them staggered over the road to the Taj Mahal Palace Hotel, opposite the Gateway of India. It was one of the most luxurious hotels in Mumbai, a fitting place to recuperate. They were greeted by attentive staff and shown to their respective suites.

Inside his room, Morgan helped Ben into one of the easy chairs by a wide window that looked out into the harbor. She rang room service and ordered chai.

"I'm not staying here," Ben said. "I want to help you."

"You've already done enough," Morgan said. She knelt by the chair and pulled him into a hug, feeling the frailty of his bones under her fingers. "I can't risk your safety again. Look at what happened to Sister Nataline."

Ben pulled away from her embrace and Morgan could see the glint of tears in his eyes. "She was calm in the moments before it happened," he said. "Her faith was so strong, not that God would somehow stop the blade from coming down, but that she would see Him soon after. She wasn't scared of death." He paused and stared out the window at the sea beyond. "I only hope that I can meet my end with such peace."

"And I hope that will be a long time," Morgan said. "Which is why I don't want you to stay. So please, go home to Oxford. Jake and I need to finish this ourselves."

Ben looked at her and Morgan felt his eyes search her own. "I'm afraid for you," he said softly. "And not just for you, but for India. These people mean to discharge the Brahmastra and they don't care about individual human lives. They think on a cosmic scale about a sacrifice so big that the gods cannot ignore them." He reached out and stroked her cheek. "I promised your mother that I would look after you and Faye and little Gemma. I fear that leaving you here will break that promise."

"Something changed for me in Rwanda," Morgan said as she stood up. "I understood why Marietti is how he is. He has seen into the heart of mass murder and he can't bear for it to happen again. If I leave with you, the chance of a disaster happening seems much greater. This may be my last ARKANE mission, because I'm not sure that the Director will ever forgive me, but I must stay."

Ben nodded. "Then I'll go home and pray for you, but you had better come back to me, Morgan."

* * *

In the next room, Jake helped Marietti to the bed. The Director sat on the edge of the soft sheet, wincing as he folded his body down. The shadows under his eyes had deepened and his hair had more white in it than Jake had noticed before.

Had he aged that much in just a few days?

"I'll ring for the doctor," Jake said. "You should be back in hospital."

Marietti shook his head. "I'm not going back there until this is over." He looked at Jake with sorrow in his eyes. "You should have stopped Morgan from retrieving that last piece. You know what we're up against. There are those, even within ARKANE, who move against me now and try to hasten disaster. This sculpture summons the end ever closer."

"You and I are shadowed men because of what we've seen, but Morgan still has hope." Jake sat down next to Marietti on the bed. "She sees a different world. The years of ARKANE have ground hope from us. We need her, we need a new perspective … We can't beat the darkness in the old ways anymore."

Marietti sighed. "Perhaps you're right. But it's getting worse, Jake. The nights I worked in the lab before the attack, I mapped a global shift in supernatural events. Signs and portents foretold for generations across many cultures are coming together, colliding and building. I fear the end of days, the great battle, may be soon upon us. We have kept so much from being revealed, but soon we will not be able to stop it spilling over."

"But we're not there yet," Jake said.

His phone buzzed with an incoming text.

"It's from Martin. He's traced the limousine." Jake stood up. "You need to rest, but I'm going with Morgan. We'll stay in touch."

CHAPTER 23

JAKE RAPPED ON THE door of Ben's room and Morgan opened it, her face expectant. Jake smiled. He had missed her even in the few minutes they were apart.

"Martin traced the limousine to a company based here," he said. "Kapoor Industries."

Morgan frowned. "That's the company of Vishal Kapoor, the man who discovered the statue with Marietti in the first place."

"Yes, and there's a daughter. Asha." Jake held out his phone so Morgan could see a picture of her face.

"It's her alright," Morgan said. "Let's go."

They headed out of the hotel and hailed an Ambassador cab. The driver darted through the downtown Mumbai traffic, Bollywood music blaring, and pulled up outside Kapoor Towers soon after.

"Martin called ahead and got us an interview with the brother," Jake said, as they walked towards the glass revolving doors into the skyscraper. "Apparently he's running the place now."

They walked into the lobby and up to reception, where a smartly dressed young woman showed them to a private lift. It zoomed them upwards and at the top they were shown into a penthouse office. Wide glass walls looked out over the dense city in one direction and out to the sea in the other.

"Magnificent, isn't it?" Mahesh Kapoor stood to greet them, walking out from behind a wide mahogany desk. "It reminds me of how insignificant we really are."

He was tall, with the looks of a Bollywood movie star and Morgan noticed how his tailored suit emphasized his muscular stature. There was a photo of his father, Vishal, on the wall, and on the desk, a framed image of a lovely young woman, presumably his wife. There was no evidence of Asha anywhere and Morgan wondered about the relationship between the siblings.

"I hear you have some information about my sister?" Mahesh said, indicating that they should sit in the leather chairs opposite his desk.

"Many years ago," Jake explained, "your father was part of an archaeological dig. They found an ancient statue of Shiva Nataraja inscribed with a sacred mantra that can invoke the Brahmastra."

Mahesh frowned. "That's a mythological weapon, only an allegory."

"No," Morgan said. "We have evidence that it has the potential to inflict mass casualties. The statue was broken apart and your father hid two pieces. The other two were hidden by Elias Marietti, his partner on the dig. Your sister has been seeking the statue and now has all four pieces. We believe she intends to invoke the weapon, but we don't know where or when."

Mahesh paced the room, his forehead creased. His frown deepened.

"Asha has been behaving strangely of late and I dismissed it as grief at our father's death." He turned to them, his arms folded, concern on his face. "But it's more than that. It's the influence of the Aghori, an extremist she follows as a guru. He has no respect for human life, believing all is illusion. He must be the one behind this."

"Either way, we need to find them. Is Asha still here?" Jake asked.

Mahesh shook his head.

"They've gone to the Kumbh Mela at Allahabad," he said.

Jake looked blank at his words.

"The Kumbh Mela is a Hindu mass pilgrimage," Morgan explained. "The largest peaceful gathering of people in one place in the world. Millions bathe at the confluence of the holy rivers Ganga, Yamuna and Sarasvati to wash away their sin. It's said that Lord Vishnu spilled drops of Amrita, the elixir of immortality, at four places while transporting it in a pot, known as a *kumbh*."

"It moves locations between those four sites and last time 120 million people visited the Kumbh," Mahesh continued, his voice soft as he realized the potential horror ahead. "Thirty million of them bathe on the most auspicious day."

The numbers were staggering. Morgan couldn't even imagine that many people in one place. But if Asha wanted a dramatic sacrifice, the Kumbh Mela would be the perfect place for it.

Mahesh bent to his computer and tapped at the keys.

"The best time to bathe is calculated by astrological positions," he said. "It will be the day after tomorrow at dawn. The sadhus, the holy men, will go first and then the mass bathing will begin. It would be carnage if a weapon were set off then. A stampede in a crowd of millions would be just as dangerous as some kind of explosion."

He paused, his frown deepening. Then, he turned the screen so Morgan and Jake could see the *Times of India* article he had found.

"They're reporting a record year at the Kumbh because of a number of miracles in rural areas," he read. "Children with the multiple arms of the goddess Kali and snakes found at sacrificial sites, with the seven heads of the *naga*. Some are claiming these are hoaxes but others are saying that it is a year of blessing and are calling for all Hindus to attend pilgrimage." He shook his head slowly. "I have my suspicions that Asha may be involved in this too. We have to find her in time. I'll put my best security men on it."

"We appreciate your help in finding her," Morgan said. "But we have also heard that there may be a way to counteract the power of the weapon. It's rumored that one of the books of the Nine Unknown may contain a counter-mantra. Do you know of this?"

Mahesh laughed, a hollow sound. "The Nine Unknown Men are equivalent to your Western Illuminati, a secret society founded by the great Emperor Ashoka in 273 BC. He had just won a battle, but the death toll was so great that he found the victory hollow and decided there had to be more to life than conquest. He searched for truths that would stand the test of time, then chose nine men and tasked each with protecting a sacred book, containing knowledge that could change mankind. Some say the books contain the elixir of immortality, the alchemists' recipe for gold, how to travel through time and even tactics of persuasion that could lead a ruler to victory."

"So what became of these books?" Jake asked.

"They are the stuff of legend," Mahesh said. "It's not even certain that they exist, and yet I know my father sought them, as have many before him and many will to come."

"Who were the Nine?" Morgan asked.

"No one knows." Mahesh walked to a bookshelf in the corner of the room and pulled out a journal. He flicked through the pages until he found the one he was looking for. "This was my father's work on the subject. Asha has been reading many of the journals he left in his room, but he gave this one to me a few years back and told me to keep it secret. He said at the time that he could no longer follow the path but that perhaps I might one day."

His fingers ran over the words. "He postulates here that not all of the Unknown Men were Indian and that influential members of society across the known world were chosen too. The tenth-century Pope Sylvester II was considered one because of his incredible knowledge of mathematics, astronomy and ancient science, way ahead of his time."

Morgan looked at Jake. "The Vatican connection explains how Ben knew about it, but how does that help us now?"

"Can we have your permission to go through that journal?" Jake asked. "We're part of an organization that researches religious and supernatural artifacts. We have a powerful database, so we could cross-reference your father's journal with some of our own information. We may be able to find hints of where the books might be."

"Of course," Mahesh said, "anything you need. While you start on that, I'll get my security staff tracking Asha."

He showed Morgan and Jake to a conference room just down the corridor from his office.

"Please, use this as your own. My resources are yours. I'll send someone to help you tap into our networks and together we'll stop my sister. My father worked his whole life to build this company, and I will not have her drag it down and use what he built for a deadly purpose."

His eyes blazed with anger as he walked out.

Minutes later, a technician came and helped them set up laptops and network access. Jake called Martin on the video phone. The ARKANE librarian sat in his office, coils of cable and old books visible in the background. They could hear the sounds of building work behind him and Martin's blond hair stood up in spikes that were far worse than usual, evidence of his stress.

"I wish you were both back here," he said. "But at least you now have Marietti and Father Ben."

Morgan knew that Martin had a soft spot for Ben after the old monk had helped him when a mission involving the Freemasons had gone horribly wrong. Martin would always be her friend, even if Marietti decided she could no longer work for ARKANE. She hoped that wasn't true, because the thought of going back to academia, to the confines of the university, filled her with dread. Her only hope was that they could stop the weapon in time.

"We need to build a custom algorithm," she said, refocusing on the work. She waved the journal at the screen. "We'll scan these pages so you have them as soon as possible to start cross-referencing. These Nine Unknown Men had sacred books with secret knowledge that could benefit mankind. Some of it was released slowly when needed, but still ahead of its time, so we should find evidence of that somehow."

Martin tapped away on his keyboard. "The ARKANE databases hook into the Vatican Secret Archives and many other sources that we probably shouldn't know about. They'll be something here."

"Tap into the Indian secret archives too," Jake said. "There's no way people haven't looked for these books already."

Martin frowned. "Actually, there's something already coming up. You're going to want to look at this."

CHAPTER 24

MARTIN SHARED HIS SCREEN with them and it filled with the image of a swastika.

"The Nazis searched for these nine books," he said. "There's a rumor that they actually found the book of psychological warfare, and that Hitler's incredible power of persuasion came from its pages."

"Any mention of weapons?" Jake asked. "Psychological warfare is one thing, but we're talking about something more immediately deadly."

"Operation Paperclip," Morgan said suddenly, her face lighting up as she recalled the details. "Of course. It was a program that took the scientists and engineers of the Third Reich and recruited them into the US and the UK in the aftermath of World War II. They officially excluded active members of the Nazi party but we know that much of the research from experiments done under the regime were used by the West. They didn't want to waste such knowledge, even though it came at the cost of so many lives."

"And the Brahmastra is fabled to have the power of a nuclear weapon," Jake said. "So, could one of the books be responsible for the development of a nuclear bomb?"

Martin tapped away again. "Oppenheimer himself researched the Nazis and talked of the Brahmastra so there was definitely a connection, but I think we need to go back even further. Some sources say that King Solomon was one of the Nine and the book of Ecclesiastes was his response to this global search for knowledge and meaning. That would make the myth a lot older than the Indian version."

"Israel is also one of the few countries with a nuclear weapon," Jake said and turned to Morgan with a cheeky grin. "Allegedly."

"Look at this," Martin interrupted. "There is an ancient group of Jews in India." He pulled up an image of a tiny synagogue with blue floor tiles beneath the golden ark of the Torah. "The Cochin Jews are said to have arrived in India with King Solomon's merchants and settled in Kerala as traders. They're also called the Malabar Jews, one of the oldest Jewish groups in India. Their local dialect still has elements of Hebrew and is known as Judeo-Malayalam."

Morgan looked at the clock on the wall.

The minutes ticked on, but they could do nothing until they had a better fix on where Asha was. If there was a chance they could find the book in time, they had to take it.

"We should go down there," she said. "It's only a couple of hours' flight to Cochin."

Jake looked doubtful, but Morgan's face lit with renewed hope.

"Remember how we met the priest on the roof of the Holy Sepulchre back in the search for the Pentecost stones? It was only by meeting him in person that he trusted us enough to tell us of the stone they had protected for generations. Perhaps if we go down to Cochin we'll find someone who can help us locate the book?"

"I can work on the database algorithm while you're doing that," Martin said.

Jake nodded. "It's worth a try."

They called the assistant that Mahesh had assigned to them and the man noted down what they needed.

"We'll have the private jet take you to Kerala within thirty minutes," he said, and turned away to make the arrangements.

They were soon on a plane heading south, the plush cabin well stocked with local and international delicacies. Morgan browsed the material that Martin had emailed over.

"The Cochin Jews share DNA with populations of some of the most ancient Jews in Ethiopia. There are also the Paradesi Jews, also called White Jews, who settled in Cochin later in the sixteenth century following the persecution in Spain and Portugal. A diaspora indeed." She shook her head. "I don't know why anyone thinks that national borders even matter anymore. We're all just hybrids from generations before."

They landed at Cochin Airport and headed for Fort Kochi, situated on the tip of a spit of land that bordered a narrow channel into the port. The taxi drove around the shoreline past the triangular nets that lined the water's edge, weighted with stones so the fishermen could cantilever them up, filled with pomfret and mackerel. The air smelled of frying fish and masala spices from street vendors who cooked the local catch for passing visitors.

A horn blared and the deep noise vibrated in Morgan's chest as a local ferry docked nearby. The taxi paused as a crowd of people emerged from the ferry and blocked the road. It was warm and humid and sweat pooled at the base of her spine, but she relished the warmth and tropical atmosphere of the place.

They drove on round the peninsula to the old quarter of Fort Kochi, known as Jew Town. It was just a few streets filled with tourist shops and the Paradesi synagogue stood at the end of one road. The street vendors called out from the low doors, offering *mezuzahs*, Hebrew calligraphy and lace, as well as Indian textiles. They were good-natured and relaxed about their pitches, a very different vibe to the intensity of Agra and Mumbai.

If only they had time to stay and look around, Morgan thought as they left their bags in a secure area, a common precaution against anti-Semitic attacks on synagogues all over the world. Jake took one of the paper *kippah*, the circular head covering for men, and placed it on as a sign of respect. They both took off their shoes and walked barefoot, the result of local Hindu influence.

"Two tickets, please," Morgan asked the woman on the door, and she felt the ticket seller's eyes scan over her. They must see a lot of tourists here every day, but Morgan knew she looked Sephardic with her dark hair, even more so as the Indian sun had brought out her skin tone.

They walked through a tiny courtyard into the synagogue itself. The floor was an unusual design of blue hand-painted porcelain tiles from China, the unique patterns drawing the eye towards the Torah ark at the front. There were a couple of information stands but mostly it was plain and simple, as the synagogues Morgan was used to back in Israel. It did feel more like a museum than a place of worship though.

An oriental rug hung on one wall and Jake walked closer to have a look.

"This is a gift from Haile Selassie, the last Ethiopian emperor," he said. "There's definitely a link with the ancient Jews here."

At the back of the room a few pamphlets about the Jews of India sat on top of a heavily protected box. Morgan picked up a leaflet as the last tourists left the room. A few moments later, the ticket seller walked in. She wore jeans and a t-shirt with a mandala on it, her long dark hair held back by a leather strip. She looked like any other young Indian woman in the area.

"That box is said to contain tenth-century copper plates," she said. "They validate the rights given to the earliest Cochin Jews and are inscribed by the ruler in Tamil." She shrugged. "I've never seen them though. Where are you from?"

"We've come from England," Morgan replied, "but I was brought up in Israel."

"Oh, it must be so different there." The young woman sighed, her eyes bright with interest. "Our community is tiny and the Cochin Jews have no Rabbis so our community is led by elders." She pointed across the room. "There's separate seating for men and women as you can see, but it seems crazy, because I'm the last female Paradesi Jew of childbearing age. There are only six Jews left living in Fort Kochi."

Jake turned at her words and Morgan understood his interest. If there were so few Jewish people left here, it was far more likely that they would discover something useful. And she could see that the woman was lonely, a prisoner of an ancient faith where intermarriage was frowned upon and yet, she had no viable choice of partner in this tiny area. There might just be a way to encourage her to open up.

"What do you think will happen to the Jewish community here in the next generation?" Morgan asked.

The woman smiled but her eyes were sad. "The graveyard is just down the road, a historical site that will be preserved for tourists. I fear that is our future. Soon we will struggle to form a minyan."

Morgan turned to Jake to explain. "A minyan is the number of Jewish adults required to perform religious obligations, usually counted as men over the age of thirteen."

She turned back to the ticket seller. "Then the knowledge of this ancient group will be lost?"

"Indeed." The woman nodded. "A fate that many ancient groups have suffered. But you're from the vibrant homeland, so as ever, the Jews are not finished and never will be. There are other Jewish communities in India too, so we're not the last footprint of the faith in this country."

"And perhaps next year in Jerusalem?" Morgan said. "I believe you'll find a welcome there if you decide to go to Israel."

"Thank you," the woman said. "It's good to meet someone with hope. I'm Rachel, by the way."

She turned to go, but Morgan reached out a hand and touched her arm lightly.

"We're looking for something related to the ancient aspects of this area. A book, rumored to have come from King Solomon himself."

Rachel paled and her jaw tightened. "I'm sorry, but I must go."

CHAPTER 25

"PLEASE WAIT," MORGAN SAID, rushing after her. "You said yourself that this generation might be the last. What's the harm in sharing now?"

Rachel turned back to them, her eyes darting warily towards the entrance.

"My father left a box," she whispered. "When he died without a son, without any male heirs, he told me to bury it and never to look inside." She looked down and blushed a little. "But I did look and I didn't bury it. There are fragile pages inside from old books."

"Can we see it?" Morgan asked, her heart beating faster with anticipation. "It's hard to explain why, but we think perhaps this book could save many lives and stop a powerful weapon from killing innocents."

Rachel smiled and shook her head.

"These stories of weapons and war, of love and death. This is India. This is what we do." She shrugged. "My own myths are woven with strands of Hinduism and Judaism. Perhaps it's time the box was shared again. I'll take my break and show you. I just live nearby."

They followed Rachel out into the street. The shop owners didn't bother them this time, merely watching as they walked past with one of their own. Rachel turned down a side alley where a few narrow buildings crammed against each other. An old woman burned rubbish at the end, a common sight where rubbish collection was rare. She poked the embers with a stick and smoke billowed out, the sweet smell of rotten vegetables filling the air.

"Please, come inside." Rachel pushed the door open. "My great aunt will be out at work, so it's just us."

Morgan and Jake walked into a room barely high enough for Jake to stand upright. He seemed to fill the space and backed into a corner while Rachel bustled around them.

She pulled a slim mattress away from the corner of the room to reveal a storage cupboard below. Jake helped her to pull the doors up and she brought out a rectangular wooden box carved with the Star of David and Hebrew script.

"This is what I was told to bury." Rachel handed it to them. "It may contain what you seek. It may not."

Morgan carried it to a low table. She and Jake sat on the floor cross-legged and opened the lid.

A smell of mildew and sawdust rose from the box. There were a stack of loose pages inside, but even without seeing them all, Morgan could see that there was no way this was part of the ancient book they sought. Some of the pages might have been a few hundred years old but it could not be one of the books of the Nine Unknown Men.

She met Jake's eyes across the table and saw her own disappointment reflected there.

Rachel came to stand near them. She folded her arms as her eyes welled with tears.

"My father protected this for his whole life," she whispered. "I don't know what to do with it all now."

Out of respect, Morgan continued to leaf carefully through the pages. There were some texts in Hebrew and others in the local Malayalam language.

"Wait," Jake said. He put his hand out to stop her. "Go back. What's that?"

It was a plain page torn out of a notebook with jagged and faded edges and a drawing in the middle. A man stood with his arms outstretched as smoke billowed from his fingertips. Beyond him was a field of corpses with roughly sketched limbs sticking up from the ground, and people fell where smoke touched them.

"That sure looks like a weapon," Jake said. "And there's something on the back."

Morgan turned the page over to find several lines of Sanskrit. Copying manuscripts had always been a way to pass down knowledge. Perhaps this was such a copy and there was no telling how old the original might have been.

"Do you mind if we take this?" she asked.

Rachel nodded. "Of course, I think my father would have been glad of your interest."

Jake's phone buzzed. He pulled it out.

"It's Mahesh. There have been sightings of Asha and the Aghori at the Kumbh Mela camp. The private jet will take us straight to Allahabad and we'll meet him there."

They stood to go. Rachel shook their hands, holding Morgan's a little longer.

"Thank you," she said. "Sometimes I forget that there's a bigger world out there, but you've given me hope."

Morgan leaned in and hugged the young woman. "Shalom berakhah ve-tovah," she whispered, a blessing of peace and good things to come.

They drove back to the airport and headed north again.

Allahabad. 7.23pm

Mahesh stood waiting next to a four-wheel drive at the airport with several more vehicles parked behind, surrounded by burly men in black sunglasses.

"Our own entourage," Jake said under his breath as they walked down the tarmac from the plane. "Not something we usually get on ARKANE missions."

"Let's just hope Asha won't see us all coming," Morgan replied, smiling at Mahesh as he approached.

He shook their hands, his face haggard with worry.

"Did you find anything in Kochi?" he asked.

"Not what we had hoped for, but it might be important." Morgan pulled out the drawing. Mahesh took it and his eyes narrowed with interest. "There's an inscription on the back."

Mahesh turned it over and his lips moved silently as he formed the words.

"You read Sanskrit?" Morgan asked.

"It's been a long time, but yes, a little, even though I don't understand the meaning in this case. The image is disturbing, though. May I keep hold of it?"

"Of course."

"How can a simple mantra be so powerful?" Jake asked, as they got into the lead vehicle.

"The Vedas teach that sound can embody power," Mahesh replied. "Mantras may have no specific meaning, but the sound itself is the reason for speaking them. Take Om, for example. It is the beginning and the end, engraved over entrances to temples and used in private prayer. The sound resonates through the chest and by repeating it you can reach a higher consciousness."

The road became densely crowded as they neared the camp, a mega city created on the banks of the Ganges, a temporary home for pilgrims who stayed only a few days as well as those who camped for the duration of the Kumbh Mela.

Eventually, the crowds became so dense that they halted the car, parking the large vehicles to the side of a couple of smaller, more rugged Jeeps.

"It gets even crazier the further we go in," Mahesh said. "So we'll leave the bigger cars here on the perimeter with a few guards."

They got into the smaller cars and drove on again. As the

crowd thickened, Mahesh ordered one of his men to walk in front with a bullhorn, clearing people out of the way but their driving speed was soon at a crawl again.

It was busy and noisy and smelled of sweating bodies and the smoke of cooking fires. The air seemed to vibrate with the excitement of the mass congregation but Morgan also felt a calm amongst the people, both a respect for life and a distance from it. The collective energy was focused only on God, on community and respect for the holy men who gathered here.

A woman in an orange sari stopped in the middle of the road before them and clutched a cell phone to her ear. She bellowed into it above the noise of the crowd, clearly trying to get directions to her part of the camp. A little boy hid in the folds of her skirt. Morgan smiled at him and he covered his face at the stranger's interest.

"The infrastructure is very well run these days," Mahesh said. "They've used urban planning principles to design camp areas, toilets, drinking water and even extra cell phone towers for coverage." He gestured at the woman on her phone. "If people can find each other easily, there is less need for help from the volunteers or police."

"Police?" Jake looked around. "We haven't seen any so far."

"Oh, they're here," Mahesh said. "But even thousands must be thinly spread in a camp this size. I've sent word to their captain and he's keeping an eye out for Asha. All the different groups of sadhus camp in separate areas so they'll check out that angle. Each group has a *mahant,* a leader, and the police will check with them first."

They passed a group of women who stood together, their hands cupped in prayer. Behind them, others jumped to the beat of a Bollywood song. "There are even female sadhus these days," Mahesh said. "Quite a few are famous now, and they have their own camps too."

"We met Asha's guru briefly," Morgan said, remembering the ash-covered man in the Kali temple.

Mahesh's face darkened and he frowned. "He's an Aghori." He spat the words. "They're ascetics dedicated to Shiva but many Hindus consider them unorthodox. They live in charnel grounds and smear ash from the dead on their skin. They drink from skulls and they use blood in their worship."

"Why would Asha choose such a path?" Morgan asked. "Surely she had everything as the only daughter of Vishal Kapoor. Why choose to follow a man like that?"

Mahesh shook his head. "I think your own scriptures explain this." His voice grew wistful. "The book of Ecclesiastes is an exploration by a young man who has everything but still finds that life is meaningless. He tries all kinds of pleasures, denying himself nothing but ultimately discovers that everything was just chasing after the wind."

"The Buddha too was a prince who gave up everything for a simpler life," Morgan said. "He renounced his riches to witness human suffering and try to transcend it."

Mahesh nodded. "Indeed, and I too have found emptiness at the heart of the rich life of Mumbai's elite. But my father taught me how to help others through our business and use wealth for good. I fear Asha has lost herself to this Aghori because she feels everything but his pure way is pointless." He looked out over the camp, the burning fires below bringing the delicious smells of spice with them. "I have failed my sister but I can still help her – if we can find her in time."

He leaned over suddenly and pressed down the horn in frustration. The blast of noise didn't even impact the crowd in front of them. Mahesh swore in Hindi, thumping his fist down onto the steering wheel.

"I'd like to walk anyway," Morgan said. "I need to stretch my legs after all that flying and it might be quicker that way."

Mahesh nodded and looked at his watch.

"I have calls to make so you should walk ahead. I have a tent booked in the front ranks nearer the water, in the section where there have been sightings of Asha and her guru. It's under the flag of a ship, the Kapoor crest. Just walk straight down the main causeway and you'll find it. If you hit the water, you've gone too far. Just call if you have any problems."

They got out the car and then Morgan leaned back in. "We'll find her in time." She met Mahesh's eyes. "We have to."

CHAPTER 26

Morgan walked with Jake along a causeway that crossed the wide river and joined the stream of pilgrims heading into the main camp area. She looked out over the shallow waters near the edge of the holy Ganges. The river was dotted with people bathing, the brown bodies and dark hair of men as they dipped under, while women in multi-colored saris managed to bathe while still preserving their modesty.

Children splashed each other and screamed with excitement. Naked sadhus painted with ash wallowed in the shallows, tinging the water white. An array of humanity all seeking to wash away sin and be closer to God, and some perhaps, just enjoying the refreshment.

Morgan watched as a man held his hands up in prayer, his eyes fixed on heaven, before he ducked under the water. As he came back up, water streaming off his face, he beamed with a look of pure rapture. She wondered whether he had traveled far and how long he had waited for that moment. It reminded her of baptism, emerging from the water to a new life. She had watched a group of Christians perform the ritual in the River Jordan once, following in the footsteps of Jesus. Water was sacred to all life so perhaps it was no surprise that it was so precious here as well.

"I'm kind of jealous," Jake said as they walked on. "I'd like to believe that washing myself in a holy river would remove all my sin." He sighed. "But the stain is too deep now."

"Then there's a Hindu story you might appreciate," Morgan said. "In the Bhagavad Gita, the great warrior Arjuna finds himself questioning what he's doing in the midst of a battle. He wants to stop and give it up because he can't see a point to the violence. Lord Krishna is with him and tells Arjuna to fight, because it is his duty and his role in life."

Morgan stopped and put her hand on Jake's arm. The sounds of the Mela fell away and in the midst of millions, they were alone. "I know some of what you've done while working for ARKANE," she whispered. "I've killed too, you know that. But we do it to protect the greater good, and if you didn't question what you did sometimes, you'd be a monster."

Jake looked down at her, his dark eyes intense, and for a moment she thought he would bend and kiss her.

And she wanted him to.

A horn blared and they both jumped. Jake pulled Morgan's arm and steered her out of the way as a Jeep piled high with pilgrims rattled past.

"We should head for Mahesh's tent before it gets dark," he said, his voice husky.

Morgan let the moment pass.

They walked down one of the avenues of the vast tent city as dusk fell, just another couple in a sea of people. The tents ranged from elaborate marquees around communal squares to the basic tarpaulin shelters of the poor. Huge banners with the faces of the gods looked down upon them, including Shiva with his trident and cobra, his hand outstretched in blessing. Flags fluttered on high rods above them, marking out the various territories within the camp and used to navigate on the paper maps clutched by new pilgrims.

The stink of cow dung used as fuel for the cook-fires hung in the air along with the smell of human bodies clustered together. There was some kind of irony that they all came to bathe, Morgan thought. Her own cotton shirt clung to her back, sweat dripping down, but she was glad of the full sleeves, long trousers and headscarf she wore. Even with her dark hair, she still stood out amongst the Indian women, although with Jake by her side, no one would bother her.

As they reached the area closest to the river, the campsites shifted from families to sadhus, mainly men, all in different groups. Morgan continued to scan the area as they walked in the hope of catching a glimpse of Asha or her Aghori, but every time she thought she saw one of them, it proved to be a mirage.

A sadhu sat outside one tent, cross-legged in the lotus position, his entire naked body and long bushy beard covered in grey ash. His dreadlocks were tied into a topknot with a marigold wreath wrapped around them and more marigolds draped around his neck and wrapped around his limbs. When so many were naked, the physical body lost its meaning and he sat so still that Morgan wondered if he was asleep.

As they passed, he opened his eyes, dark pools against the ash on his skin. She put her hands together in the prayer position and bent towards him.

"Namaste."

The sadhu nodded back. She found these men alien after coming from Judaism where physical modesty was valued and the holy men spent hours at their books.

Another tent a little further down was alive with discussion, groups of sadhus gesticulating as they conversed of sacred things. The tent was smoky from their *chillum* pipes, the sweet scent of marijuana hanging in the air. Morgan smiled. Perhaps they weren't so different to the Rabbis who spent years arguing over the finer points of the Torah.

The sky darkened as night fell, but it only became brighter as they reached the camp area closer to the river. Shrines were lit up with lanterns and vehicles passed by, alive with festive electric lights and stereos blaring sacred chants. The yellow glow of the streetlamps all served to create an eerie form of night.

"There." Jake pointed up ahead to where a flag flapped in the breeze. "The Kapoor ship."

They walked to it and pushed open the flap of an ivory-colored marquee, an oasis of calm and cool after the mayhem outside.

Mahesh had commandeered a large tent with separate areas for sleeping and a lounge area for visitors. The festival was a chance to eat together and meet family and friends, as well as worship. A time to celebrate what made life truly worth living, away from the grind of working a city office job or tilling the fields in rural India.

Of course, some could do it in style, Morgan thought, and this tent was a world away from the simple tarpaulin shelters they had seen in the areas further out. Mahesh's assistant brought them cold drinks from the fridge. Sometimes a sweet, fizzy soda was the best thing on earth. Morgan drank deeply.

Mahesh unrolled an aerial map of the camp on the table and pinned the corners down. Morgan and Jake gathered around.

"I got this from one of the news helicopters earlier."

Even at a tiny scale, the camp was huge, stretching for miles in both directions along the banks of the river. It was incredible to imagine the number of individual pilgrims massed in each quadrant, many having come from all over India and from abroad, linked by their desire to commune with God and receive forgiveness for their sin.

Morgan's own belief was complicated. Raised as a Jew by her father in Israel but not Jewish because her mother was Christian, she had always sat on the edge of faith and her work as a psychologist only served to make her question further. But she had seen the supernatural made real in her work with ARKANE, and that kept her seeking. Part of her wanted to believe that the Brahmastra weapon was only a myth, but she had gazed into the Gates of Hell not so long ago and she knew that the darkness was never far away.

"The Aghori sect roam alone through India but there are reports they are congregating around here." Mahesh pointed at one area of the map. "I have men there giving alms to the sadhus and watching for female pilgrims but I believe we should go and search for ourselves." He frowned and rubbed at his forehead in anguish. "If I can only get to my sister …"

Morgan put her hand on his arm. "We still have time."

As they readied themselves to go out into the camp again, the flap of the tent opened and a young boy poked his head in.

"Mr Kapoor," he said. "Delivery, sir." He walked further in with a large cardboard box, sent by courier from Delhi.

Mahesh took it and gave the boy some rupees. He looked at the label and then handed it to Jake.

"It's for you."

Jake grinned as he put the box on the table. "Excellent. This will help a lot." He tore open the package to reveal a quadcopter drone with a camera that could be attached on the mount underneath. The four rotors meant it was easily maneuverable and could be flown by an app on Jake's smart phone. "I got Martin to sort one out via the Delhi office." He focused on fiddling with the controls. "It'll help us search the crowd more easily."

"Even at night?" Morgan asked.

"Oh, don't worry about that," Mahesh said. "This place is alive by night with fires and torches. If anything, it's busier when it's not so hot, and anything is worth a try at this point."

Jake fitted the battery pack and camera.

"All fully charged and ready to go. You don't even have to actively fly these ones. It can follow the signal from my phone and fly above us as we walk." He grinned, looking every inch the schoolboy with a new toy.

Morgan itched to try it herself, but she knew she wouldn't get a chance while Jake held the controls. It was good to see him smile though, even as the hours counted down to the dawn.

They walked out of the tent into the sprawl of the camp. There were fires every few meters, casting a golden glow over the faces of the pilgrims. Women squatted cooking dinner for their families as the smell of cardamom and curry leaves filled the air. Children ran around, squealing in excitement as they met new friends. It was a social scene, eating and drinking together that was common the world over, in every culture. But as they walked towards the fires of the sadhus, the camp became more alien again.

A group of naked *naga* sadhus sat around a fire, one of them fanning smoke over the rest as they sat in meditation, suffering the heat and fumes in order to transcend physical sensation.

Mahesh led Morgan and Jake onwards towards the Aghori camp, which was nearer the water. Despite the crush of humanity in the area, there were no tents anywhere near their fires. The sect lived as outcasts as they traveled, sleeping in charnel grounds and embracing taboo. Even here they were pushed to the edge of the civilized world. It was eerily quiet and the hum of the camp seemed to fade behind them.

There were no overhead lights and as they walked closer, Morgan realized that most of the Aghori sat around several larger fires, eyes fixed on the flames. They were skeletal thin, sustained by discarded rubbish, eating rotten human flesh and drinking the blood of animal sacrifice from their *kapala* skull bowls.

Mahesh weaved his way around the campfires, gazing at the figures around each of them in turn. Morgan followed him, a few paces behind, as Jake stood back a few meters, checking the drone settings.

A moan rose up from one of the men, turning to a wail

as he began to shake and convulse. Mahesh kept walking, scanning for Asha's guru, but Morgan couldn't help but stay and watch for a moment. The other sadhus ignored the man now writhing on the ground as he kicked his heels into the fire. Surely he would burn.

"Lord Shiva comes." The harsh whisper was close. "Kali Ma comes."

Morgan turned quickly to find one of the Aghori right behind her. His breath stank of rotten flesh and his teeth were stained from the *chillum* pipe and the blood of sacrifice. He had bones woven through his long dreadlocks and his body was dusted with ash.

His eyes were glazed, like he was in some kind of trance state or just intoxicated by the alcohol that was part of the Aghori ritual. He held a live chicken in one hand and it squawked as it flapped in his fist. He stepped towards Morgan, backing her towards the fire.

"If we do not offer everything to Kali Ma," he hissed, "we cannot receive her blessing. Only by sacrifice can the world be saved."

Morgan couldn't see Jake or Mahesh anymore. The fires around her filled her vision with flame and she could see it reflected in the Aghori's eyes. The river had faded to black and the sky above lit with blood. Smoke swirled about her, acrid with some kind of herb. She felt dizzy and looked around, suddenly disorientated.

A low chanting began and she saw the other men were now staring at her, some rising to their feet to come closer. Morgan held herself steady even as her heart pounded with fear. There were so many of them.

"Is there a woman here?" she stammered, her voice hoarse from the smoke. "Asha Kapoor. She follows one of your own."

The sadhu leaned towards her and the stink of shit and rotten flesh rose from his skin.

"Only you and the goddess are here tonight," he whispered and bared his teeth. "And she demands sacrifice."

He gripped her arm, his fingers strong and wiry.

Morgan tried to pull away but suddenly, there were naked sadhus all around, pressing their stinking bodies against her as they called to the gods.

There were too many of them and she spun around, pushing them, trying to get away. She was dizzy from the smoke, nausea rising as she tried to scream.

One of the sadhus pushed her and she fell forward onto her knees. The Aghori raised the squawking chicken above her head and held it by the neck.

Then he bent and bit into it, his teeth ripping the flesh away as its blood spurted out.

CHAPTER 27

Morgan felt warmth spatter her face. The copper stink of fresh blood and the sweet intensity of the smoke and the rising chant of the Aghori filled her mind.

In the shadows beyond, she thought she saw a woman with skin the color of a thundercloud and eyes of flame. In her outstretched hand was the bloody head of Sister Nataline, and around her body was a girdle of skulls.

"Kali," Morgan whispered, as the goddess stalked towards her, raising her kukri high above her head.

Then Morgan felt hands on her body and at the edge of unconsciousness, she heard a scream, her own voice in the darkness.

"No!"

Suddenly the Aghori scattered as a huge man loomed from the darkness, fists flying as he shoved the skinny sadhus away. Moments later, Morgan was in Jake's arms and he was half-carrying, half-dragging her away from the campfires.

Back in the light and bustle of the main camp, he lay her on the ground. They were soon surrounded by people clamoring for a look but Morgan didn't care. She focused on Jake's face and tried to banish the horror of what she had seen.

"I'm so sorry." He dabbed at her skin, wiping the chicken's blood off as he held her close with the other arm. "I lost you in the smoke, just for a minute. Then I heard you scream." Jake looked at her, his features creased with concern. "What did you see?"

"I … I thought I saw–"

"What happened?" Mahesh burst through the crowd, then turned and shouted in Hindi for the onlookers to move away. "Oh goodness, Morgan, are you hurt?"

Morgan shook her head. "No, just a little lightheaded. That's some powerful smoke they have there. It's not my blood. The Aghori sadhus had some kind of ritual sacrifice and I stumbled into it."

A look of disgust crossed Mahesh's face. "As Kali drank the blood of the demon Raktabija, so they drink the blood of sacrifice."

"We need to get you back to the tent," Jake said, his arms still wrapped around Morgan, shielding her from the crowd around. She wanted to close her eyes and rest in his warmth, let herself be protected. The attack had been shocking, but had she really seen the dark goddess in the smoke?

Mahesh looked at his watch. "We're almost out of time. They'll start organizing the march down to the river soon. The *naga* sadhus will go first at dawn and then everyone else will mass behind."

Morgan pushed Jake away, stood, and brushed the dirt from her clothes to hide the shaking in her hands. The stink of blood brought bile to her throat. "I'm fine, really. I just need to go and change quickly. I'll meet you back here."

"I'll come with you," Jake said.

"There's no time. I'll be quick."

Mahesh turned and indicated the causeway that crossed part of the river where the main bathing would happen.

"We'll be up there. It's the best vantage point."

Fingers of pink and orange crept into the sky above the camp as Morgan picked her way back through the crowd to Mahesh and Jake after changing. The brief time alone had given her breathing space and she pushed the experience to the back of her mind. Dwelling on it only reinforced the memory, but she still found herself clenching her fists as the dark images resurfaced. She hurried up to the causeway where they had a view over the massed millions, a crush of people stretching way back from the shore.

Dawn was only minutes away now.

And still, they had nothing.

Jake flew the drone above the heads of the crowds, while Mahesh and Morgan scanned the faces on screen for a glimpse of Asha or her Aghori.

"There!" Mahesh said.

Jake circled the drone back for another pass, focusing on the woman he had seen.

"No, damn it, that's not her." Mahesh's voice was desperate now.

A roar came up from the crowd as they parted for the first group of *naga* sadhus, naked but for their ashes and garlands of marigolds. Many carried the trident of Shiva as they marched down to the waters, shouting to the gods as they arrived to bathe at the most auspicious time.

The waters looked dark and forbidding and Morgan found her gaze drawn out to those pilgrims who avoided the crush to bathe from boats in the current. Then she caught a glimpse of white ash against the fading night.

"Out there," she said, pointing at a boat that stood out from the rest of the tourist vessels. It had a metal hull with an outboard engine, and it was elaborately decorated with flowers and paintings of Shiva in his resplendent dance of time. The Aghori stood tall at the prow, his dark skin now white with ash. He held his *kapala* human skull to the sky and his lips moved in a mantra. Next to him sat a woman, her head covered in a saffron-colored scarf.

Jake zoomed the drone towards them, focusing in on the woman's face as she turned to look at what buzzed above.

"Asha," Mahesh whispered, and in his bereft tone, Morgan knew he faced the reality of what his sister had become.

In the frame of the drone's camera, Asha's eyes widened.

"She knows we're here," Mahesh said. "It's only minutes before the alignment. We must get to them." He signaled at his bodyguards and ran towards them. "Get me a boat now!"

"See if you can use the drone to slow them down," Morgan said and then ran after Mahesh, down towards the shore.

* * *

Jake focused on the screen as he tried to shut out the noise of the mass of pilgrims around him. He zoomed the drone down over the Aghori's head, buzzing past Asha and the sadhu. But the holy man ignored the noise, standing unmoved as the seconds ticked past.

At the moment of confluence, when the most auspicious time arrived, the tone of the crowd changed to one of reverence. Some shouted with excitement, others cried out to the gods and still more fell to their knees in silence, crawling towards the water to wash away their sins.

In the tiny camera screen, Jake watched as Asha reached for the Shiva Nataraja sculpture, now fully complete.

They were out of time.

He panned the camera out. Mahesh and Morgan were in a powerboat now, fighting their way through the mass of craft on the water, but they were too far away to do anything.

Asha handed the sculpture to the Aghori and he began to read the ancient mantra on its side, calling the power of the gods down and channeling it through him.

Jake watched his lips move and for a moment, it seemed as if they had worried for nothing.

But then the air crackled and shifted.

A sudden hot wind surged, whipping the river into waves. The clouds above whirled into a vortex in hues of ash and pitch and a veil of gloom obscured the pink of dawn as it began to rain, great thick drops that pelted the crowd.

Pilgrims raised their hands to heaven, calling out their prayers as they turned their faces to the sky in expectation.

Then the screaming started.

CHAPTER 28

THE RIVER BOILED, ITS temperature spiking as the Aghori spoke the ancient words. Steam rose as cold rain hit the waves and mist made it harder to see in the semi-darkness. Screams of agony rang through the air and those in deeper waters scrambled for the shore, pushing others under in their haste to get out. But there were so many people crushed into every inch of water that they were trapped as the panic widened.

The faithful crumpled into the waves as their flesh boiled, the animal cries of the dying echoing above the pilgrim throng. In the confusion, those on the shore were pushed towards the boiling waters by those behind. The Aghori held the sculpture to his chest and his chant intensified. Then he cupped his hands as if to push the energy from him and shouted his mantra to the sky as he flung his hands towards the shore.

The air boomed as a wave of boiling water rushed away from him, steam rising into the air in billowing clouds and expanding circles. The wave crashed down onto the pilgrims on the shore, crushing them and roasting them as they died. He chanted on and Asha stood by his side, her face ecstatic at the sacrifice.

A miasma rose up, a fog of rolling death that crept over the waves towards the shore. As it touched the crowd massed by the edge of the water, they began to scream as they tore at their clothes. Their flesh melted at its touch and their bodies burned down to bone before they crumpled on the ground.

Morgan looked around in horror at the carnage on the shore, the bodies that bobbed in the boiling water, but this could only be the beginning.

There were millions more in the camp and the burning mist was heading for them all.

The Aghori took a breath as he prepared for another round and he raised the sculpture again.

"Ram them!" Morgan shouted. "We have to stop him chanting."

Mahesh looked back towards the shore to see the rolling mist intensify, its power growing with every repetition of the mantra.

"It's too late," he whispered, his voice desolate.

"It's never too late," Morgan said. She nudged him aside and took the wheel, angling the boat across the river as she accelerated.

Then she remembered the sketch from Fort Kochi.

"Try the Sanskrit on the back of the drawing," she shouted above the wind.

Mahesh moved to the port side of the boat, fighting to keep his balance as he pulled the slip of paper from his pocket, holding it with both hands as he began to read.

"*Dalla hava mahey mum, yastra hala duvestra hum.*"

His voice was hesitant at first but Morgan felt a shiver at his words. The hairs on the back of her neck stood up and even though she couldn't understand the phrase, she felt the air shift.

Mahesh recited the mantra again, this time with more confidence as the words rolled from his tongue in powerful syllables.

The Aghori faltered and his arms dropped as the counter-mantra touched him. The boiling mist before him softened and sank towards the water.

Asha turned and saw the approaching boat, her brother standing on the prow.

"No!" she screamed.

Morgan rammed into them.

The impact of metal against metal sounded like a gong above the noise of the screaming crowd. Morgan slammed into the deck and slid towards the stern as the boat crumpled at a steep angle but Mahesh scrambled up and over the bow with a roar, leaping onto the other boat as he shouted the Sanskrit phrase in triumph.

The Aghori cowered, covering his ears as Mahesh leapt upon him. They tussled, rolling together, both screaming their ancient words.

Mahesh lunged and they both fell together over the side. The two men sank down into the dark depths of the river, wrestling together even as they writhed in agony in the boiling water, their skin loosening from their flesh as they drowned.

The sound of wailing came from the shore as those still alive mourned their desperate loss. The river swirled with dead corpses and amongst them, Mahesh Kapoor and the Aghori, their bodies twisted together in death.

Asha rushed to the side, reaching down towards the men, her face stricken with loss. For the Aghori. For her brother. For the end of her dreams of sacrifice.

But the men were gone.

Asha turned back to the other boat, her eyes fixed on Morgan. "What have you done?" she screamed. Morgan saw the rage of the goddess in her eyes and realized that Asha still had the sculpture of Shiva Nataraja.

This wasn't over yet.

Morgan reached up, straining to pull herself towards the other boat. But Asha spun and started the engine, revving away so her boat pulled into the current. Her own craft was ruined and Morgan could only watch Asha speed away as the waters calmed. She would soon be out of sight and they would lose her.

Then the drone buzzed overhead.

Hope rose within her, providing renewed energy to continue the chase. Jake could track Asha from above. They could still get the sculpture back.

"Please help me!" Morgan called to the nearest boat. They pulled alongside and helped her in, making sure she didn't touch the steaming water, discolored with human flesh and blood.

The haunted faces of the men in the boat betrayed their shock at what had happened. They spoke to her in their language, and although she couldn't understand the words, she knew what they were saying. The words of grief were universal. She could only nod as they took her back to shore.

As soon as the boat touched bottom, Morgan jumped out and the men headed back out again to help others, or at least bring in more bodies. She ran back along the shore towards the causeway. Jake still stood there, concentrating on the screen, and she could see his hands moving as he directed the drone in pursuit.

She hurried to him, wanting to fall into his arms, needing his support after the horror of the waters below.

"Are you alright?" he said, his voice curt as he concentrated. As ever, there was too much to say and no time to say it.

Morgan looked over his shoulder at the tiny screen on his phone. The drone's camera was still focused on Asha's boat as she headed east.

"Mahesh is gone," she whispered.

"I saw," Jake said. "But he saved millions here today." He zoomed in on Asha's figure. She held the wheel of the powerboat but she slumped against it, her body drooping. "And she is almost finished. Look how broken she is."

"I don't know," Morgan said. "I saw her rage when the Aghori and Mahesh went over the side. She was not just a follower, she's strong. Legend says that the Brahmastra can only be used one time before it needs to recharge, but if we can't catch her, she may try again another time. But at least we're tracking her."

Jake shook his head. "We have a little problem there." He nodded at the screen and Morgan saw the battery indicator was at one bar. "We probably have about twenty minutes left and then the drone will be out of power. I'll stay on her as long as possible but once the drone drops out of the sky, we'll be blind."

Morgan pulled out her own smart phone, navigating to the maps and tracing the river's path.

"The Ganges weaves east to Varanasi," she said. "The holiest city for Hindus. There are cremation ghats, steps on the edge of the river, where they burn bodies day and night. Asha would find other Aghori there and also temples to Shiva and Kali."

"It's our best bet," Jake said. "And we have to try something. I'll stay on her with the drone while you go get a vehicle and we'll head there by road."

Morgan jogged back to the Kapoor tent. Mahesh's assistant stood at the open door, gazing out into the chaos of the crowd as he wrung his hands together in anxiety. The sound of wailing and chanting rose like a prayer to heaven and mist swirled above the heads of the pilgrims, dank with the stench of burned bodies.

"This is terrible, Miss Morgan," he said, shaking his head. "Have you seen Mr Kapoor?"

Morgan took a deep breath and put her hand on his arm.

"I'm so sorry. Mahesh is out there, amongst the people he served – you'll need to retrieve his body. He gave his life to save others."

The man fell to his knees, his face stricken, his hands clasped together and eyes to heaven. He began to pray, his lips moving in ritual prayers for the dead.

Morgan ducked inside the tent. There was no time to

mourn while Asha still held the sculpture, and after seeing what the Aghori were capable of, the thought of the weapon falling into their hands was terrifying.

She grabbed the keys to one of the four-wheel-drive vehicles they had left further out on the perimeter. It would be quicker to get out there on foot rather than try to drive out, especially as the camp was in convulsions.

The shouts of police could be heard above the sounds of mourning as they tried to gain control. But the camp was a collective body, mortally wounded, and its suffering seemed to flow across the millions gathered as word spread of death in the holy waters.

Morgan left the tent again, stopping next to Mahesh's assistant.

"I'm sorry but I have to go. Please radio the men at the vehicles further out that I'm coming to take one. We're tracking Asha Kapoor east. She's responsible for this terrible crime."

The man nodded. "Of course, and I know that Mr Kapoor would have wanted me to help you." Tears welled in his eyes. "I must speak to his widow."

Morgan jogged back to Jake. He stood in the same place, but now he gazed down at the bodies lying on the shore below. He clutched the railing, his knuckles white with tension.

He turned as she approached, his dark eyes full of sorrow. Morgan walked into his arms and they embraced. She felt the warmth of his body, heard the beating of his heart.

"I don't know how many more times I can see this," he whispered, his lips against her hair. "Every time I think we're close to some kind of victory, we leave so many dead behind."

"It could have been many more," Morgan said. She tightened her arms around him, pulling him closer. "And we have a chance to finish this now."

Jake stepped back and ran his hands through his hair as he pulled himself together. "OK, let's do this. The drone ran out of power and dropped into the river but she's definitely still on the boat, heading east. In the meantime, Martin's going to see if he can get a satellite lock on her position."

Morgan held out the keys. "We need to get back to the vehicles on the perimeter and then we can head after her. Even though we're behind, the road will be faster. We could still make it to Varanasi before Asha and intercept her on the ghats by the river."

CHAPTER 29

As the river wound away from Allahabad, the sounds of mourning faded and eventually, Asha could only hear the slap of water on the hull. She looked out towards the villages on the banks of the Ganges. A woman squatted on a rock doing her washing. A herd of water buffalo munched in the shallows. Men worked in the fields, their laughter and good-natured chatter rippling out towards her. The sounds of rural India, a background to life that she had never known growing up in the craziness of Mumbai and the privilege of wealth.

Maybe if she had grown up out here, she would have found love and had a family, a simpler life that may have satisfied her. But she would never know those pleasures now.

Asha sighed and brushed away the tears from her cheeks. She had lost her brother to the boiling waters along with her guru. The other dead pilgrims meant nothing to her, but those two men had been precious and their loss cut to her heart.

The goddess had asked for a sacrifice, but perhaps her demand had never been for pilgrims. Perhaps she had only ever wanted Asha's dearest, or perhaps the timing had just not been right.

She looked down at the sculpture of Shiva Nataraja, the bronze glinting as the sun rose higher in the sky. If the carving truly was the Brahmastra mantra, she could use it again.

And it wouldn't have to be in India.

She could take it to London or New York, anywhere the casualties might be even higher than the Kumbh Mela.

A piercing cry rang out over the river. She looked up to see a peacock on the edge of the bank, its feathers spread in a perfect semi-circle of brilliant blues and purple.

It stared right at her, its piercing eyes glinting as it screeched again.

"Mayura," Asha whispered, the Sanskrit word for peacock. The bird was sacred to Hindu mythology, depicted as killing a snake, the symbol of the cycle of time. Was it meant to be a warning?

Confusion swept over her. What did the goddess want?

She had to get to the Aghori in Varanasi. She would join their rite and in the blood and the fire, she would see the goddess again and learn her true wishes.

* * *

Morgan and Jake drove into the outskirts of Varanasi. The highway had been swift but as they wove through the streets into the central city, it became useless to drive any further.

Skinny cows with jutting ribs wandered the streets chewing on whatever they could find, as birds of prey wheeled overhead. A woman squatted next to the road with a tray of pomegranates, one split open to show the red flesh inside. A flower seller with marigolds spattered by the rain hawked his wares next to jasmine flowers and huge gourd-like cucumbers, dried coconut and piles of colorful dye for offerings. The sound of horns and radios playing Bollywood tunes filled the air, blaring horns and bells and the crush of pilgrims overwhelming anyone who stood still. A scooter zoomed past driven by a man with his wife and three children plus a chicken piled around him.

"Something like that would be much faster," Jake said as they sat in a traffic jam.

"Let's do it," Morgan said.

They left their vehicle at the side of the road and hailed a bicycle rickshaw.

"Where to, ma'am?" the young driver asked, his bare feet ready on the pedals.

"Is there a temple to the goddess Kali on the ghats?" Morgan asked.

"There is a shrine near Dashashwamedh Ghat. I will take you there?"

Morgan nodded. "Yes, please."

He darted down a side street and into the warren of the ancient city, ringing his bell as he clattered along. Morgan held onto the side of the cart, leaning into Jake to try and avoid getting slammed into the walls as the young man rounded corners at speed.

They shot through an intersection, weaving in between sacred cows and buses filled with people. The traffic was like a shoal of fish, moving together, inches apart and yet somehow not colliding, as if a sixth sense sparked between them. Decorated trucks with multi-colored paintings and tinsel bore down on their tiny vehicle but at the last minute the driver swerved, grinning back at them in triumph.

"Look at the damn road," Jake shouted. He turned to Morgan. "Maybe you have to see life as cyclical here, so you can stop worrying about dying every five minutes."

The city was dirty and dusty and the buildings drooped into one another as if they might tumble like dominos any minute. But despite the dense humanity packed in like sardines, there was a pervading sense of calm. This place was truly sacred and to die here meant an escape from the circle of reincarnation. For if the ashes of the dead floated in the Ganges at Varanasi, the soul would ascend to heaven with no need to come back to the agony of life. Some days, Morgan could see why such a belief would be so precious.

After a short journey, they paid the driver and walked

down onto the ghat. Sadhus sat in lotus position on the bank, their backs straight and bodies still as they stared at the horizon. Beggars held tins out as Morgan and Jake passed. They asked for a few rupees for firewood for their own pyres, because it took a great deal to burn a human corpse to dust. Even death was hard here.

Near the steps of the ghat, a man drove his buffalo herd into the water and began to wash them, while just downstream, a dhobi-wallah washed a pile of clothes, slapping the bright material on the steps. A woman stood in the shallows, weeping as she released a wreath of flowers onto the holy waters.

Morgan and Jake found the Kali shrine in a parade of other gods, her black face and red tongue as well as the severed heads marking her out. Pilgrims prayed next to it, leaving flowers and other offerings. The sound of prayer cymbals and the smell of incense emanated from the shrine.

But they couldn't spot Asha in the crowd of pilgrims.

Jake's phone buzzed.

"Martin says that the satellite shows she definitely alighted from the boat here at Varanasi, but further downstream at the burning ghats."

"That's the cremation grounds where the Aghori would congregate too," Morgan said. "Let's head in that direction."

Shadows lengthened as they walked along the edge of the river, and when they eventually reached one of the main cremation ghats, it was getting dark. The pyres burned here twenty-four hours a day, seven days a week, to process the huge numbers of dead, and as they walked through, Morgan glimpsed the different stages of cremation.

A group of men carried a body down to a pyre that was stacked high, ready for burning. The corpse was wrapped in orange silk and garlanded with flowers. The men lifted it high and placed it onto the wood and a young man leaned forward to light the kindling, his face contorted with grief.

Later, he would have to crack the skull of the dead to release its spirit, but for now, he bore witness to the end of another life.

Flames hissed and popped and the sound of sonorous bells rang through the air. The heat was intense and as they wove through the fires, Morgan was reminded of the story of the furnace of Nebuchadnezzar, when three young Jews walked in the flames unhurt because of their faith in God. This was a primal place and staring into the flames here meant watching a human body return to bone and ashes.

"There," Jake whispered suddenly.

Towards the end of the ghat, in the shadows beyond the main pyres, a group of Aghori sat in front of a huge fire. They sat so close that it seemed impossible that their skin didn't burn. Their *kapala* skulls sat before them, bone glinting in the flickering light and the ash on their naked bodies marked them out in the darkness.

Between the men, Jake and Morgan saw the smaller figure of a woman.

They approached slowly, weaving between the fires until they reached the perimeter of the Aghori circle. One of the sadhus looked up at them with dark eyes.

Morgan was wary after her experience at Allahabad and she could smell the sweet smoke that had blinded her back then. The *kapala* skulls were filled with blood and ritual alcohol and the men would be intoxicated as they sought the way to the goddess.

Asha sat within the circle, surrounded by Aghori sadhus. The sculpture of Shiva Nataraja sat between her crossed legs and she stared into the fire. Her eyes were glazed and she seemed to be in a trance. The blood of animal sacrifice marked her face, daubed in thick clots and scattered with ash.

A bell rang out, its dull note sounding three times.

The Aghori began to chant.

Asha's face changed and tears welled, dripping down her face as she wept in anguish, leaving trails through the blood and ash.

She swayed in place as the Aghori's chant grew louder, and changed to a repetitive mantra of harsh words, guttural and raw. One of them offered his *kapala* skull to her and she drank deep, her head tipped back as she finished the bowl of bloody alcohol.

The Aghori rose and Asha stood with them, her eyes fixed on the flames. She held the statue of Shiva tight against her chest.

Suddenly Morgan saw her intention.

"No," she whispered and stepped forward, her hands outstretched.

But the Aghori closed ranks, protecting the circle as Asha walked into the ring of fire and sank down into the circle of wood. She made no sound at first, her eyes glazed over as the chanting rang through the air.

Then the flames pierced her consciousness. She threw her head back and screamed.

Morgan tried to fight her way into the circle.

"Let me help her," she begged, but the Aghori blocked her path, their wiry muscles strong and unmoving.

"It's no use," Jake said, his hand gentle on her arm. "She made her choice."

They watched as Asha's skin blackened and she crumpled to a heap, mercifully out of sight. The corpse crackled as the Aghori fed the flames.

Through a crack in the piled timber, Morgan caught a glimpse of the bronze statue as the metal flames surrounding Shiva danced in the heat of true fire. The etchings of the mantra carved into the statue rippled in the heat and the words dissolved into one another.

"Look," Morgan whispered, pointing it out to Jake. "The weapon can't be invoked again. At least not that way."

He nodded and took her hand. "Now Asha is dead and gone, I don't want to see what the Aghori do with her body."

Morgan shuddered at the thought of their cannibal rituals. "You're right. It's time to go home. There's just one more thing I want to do."

CHAPTER 30

MORGAN AND JAKE STOOD on the edge of the Ganges looking east as the sun rose over the horizon and cast a fiery trail across the water.

"How quickly things change," Morgan said. "Yesterday we stood waiting for the dawn with Mahesh and now he's gone. Asha's dead, and so many more are with their gods."

"And we're still standing," Jake said. "Be thankful for that, because one day, you or I will stand alone." He took her hand and kissed it, his dark eyes intense as he looked at her. "I hope that won't be for a long time."

Together, they crouched next to the water and lit tea lights inside little cardboard boats, used to carry prayers onto the sacred waters. They sprinkled marigolds around the flames and pushed them gently into the current.

Morgan put her hands together in the prayer position over her heart.

"Namaste," she whispered, her thoughts with Mahesh. They watched until the little lights were lost in the encroaching dawn.

"Let's go home," Jake said.

Hours later, as the plane took off, Morgan looked down at the city of Varanasi as it grew smaller beneath them. She pressed her nose to the window so she could drink in that last look and then it was gone, lost below the clouds.

Jake was already on the edge of sleep, his eyes closed, a

shutter against the world. But Morgan felt a strange sense of loss as they headed west. People had traveled to India for generations seeking meaning and enlightenment. There was even a myth that Jesus had not died on the cross, but ended up here instead. Those who stayed in the country could spend a lifetime looking for meaning, and some lucky few found what they sought. But those who left could not forget, and India lingered, like the scent of a lover.

Morgan suddenly felt the truth of that and longed to stay, to immerse herself in the rich culture, the colors and extremity of experience that made her feel so alive. India was like Israel in that way, a place on the edge of life and death where an unexpected turn in the road could take you into the heart of an ancient ruin or the hands of a mob. The very unpredictability of it was part of the thrill.

India was full of life and laughter and people here lived in the moment, because who knew what tomorrow would bring.

She would come back here. She was sure of it.

Morgan closed her eyes and let sleep come.

London, England.

Morgan and Jake slipped into the city before dawn and arrived in Trafalgar Square by taxi from Heathrow Airport.

"Terrible thing that bombing," the cabbie said, shaking his head as he took their fare. "But look at how quickly it's all been rebuilt. The terrorists can't crush Londoners."

The square was quiet as they walked beneath the facade of the National Gallery. The reconstruction was well underway, with the square rebuilt and the fountains almost finished. Nelson's Column stood proud again and although the lions closest to the blast area were still missing, they would be rebuilt soon enough. No one would ever notice the difference and within months, the city would forget, its attention distracted by the latest headlines.

They entered ARKANE through the basement of St Martin-in-the-Fields church, going through multiple levels of security including new biometric scanning.

Morgan held her breath as she faced the machines, still wary of Marietti's anger at her actions. But it beeped green and they walked together down through the lab area towards Martin's office.

"Morgan, Jake. Wait." The voice boomed through the corridor and they turned to see Director Marietti at the entrance to one of the labs. He held a cane and rested against the door frame, his body still weak from his injuries. But his eyes were steel hard. He would not back down in the face of danger, whether inside ARKANE or out in the world.

Jake went to him and embraced his mentor, then stepped back, aware that he had overstepped the mark. But Marietti smiled.

"It's good to see you back safely." He looked at Morgan. "Both of you."

His eyes met hers. It was as close to an apology as she was likely to get. And that was OK.

"I know you've just returned but there's something we need to work on together." He beckoned them into the lab, where Martin Klein stood next to an artifact on a bench. "Something that threatens us all."

* * *

The adventures continue for the
ARKANE team in *End of Days*, available now.

The thousand years are ended.

A marble tablet found in the ruins of Babylon warns of the resurrection of a banished serpent in the final days. A sarcophagus is discovered in the deepest ocean, locked by seven seals scattered throughout the ancient world.

As the Brotherhood of the Serpent race to find the seals before a rare lunar eclipse over the heart of Jerusalem, ARKANE agents Morgan Sierra and Jake Timber battle to find them first.

But this time, evil threatens to destroy all that Morgan loves and she must wrestle an apocalyptic foe as well as fighting to conquer her own darkest fears.

In a fast-paced adventure from the ruins of Iraq to the snake-handling churches of the Appalachian Mountains, from archaeological digs in Israel to the tombs of Egypt, Morgan and Jake must find the seven seals and stop the resurrection of an evil as old as mankind. An evil that will usher in the End of Days.

ENJOYED DESTROYER OF WORLDS?

If you loved the book and have a moment to spare, I would really appreciate a short review on the page where you bought the book. Your help in spreading the word is gratefully appreciated and reviews make a huge difference to helping new readers find the series. Thank you!

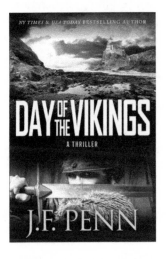

Get a free copy of the bestselling thriller, *Day of the Vikings*, ARKANE book 5, when you sign up to join my Reader's Group. You'll also be notified of new releases, giveaways and receive personal updates from behind the scenes of my thrillers.

WWW.JFPENN.COM/FREE

* * *

Day of the Vikings, an ARKANE thriller

A ritual murder on a remote island under the shifting skies of the aurora borealis.

A staff of power that can summon Ragnarok, the Viking apocalypse.

When Neo-Viking terrorists invade the British Museum in London to reclaim the staff of Skara Brae, ARKANE agent Dr. Morgan Sierra is trapped in the building along with hostages under mortal threat.

As the slaughter begins, Morgan works alongside psychic Blake Daniel to discern the past of the staff, dating back to islands invaded by the Vikings generations ago.

Can Morgan and Blake uncover the truth before Ragnarok is unleashed, consuming all in its wake?

Day of the Vikings is a fast-paced, supernatural thriller set in London and the islands of Orkney, Lindisfarne and Iona. Set in the present day, it resonates with the history and myth of the Vikings.

If you love an action-packed thriller,
you can get Day of the Vikings for free now:

WWW.JFPENN.COM/FREE

Day of the Vikings features Dr. Morgan Sierra from the ARKANE thrillers, and Blake Daniel from the London Crime Thrillers, but it is also a stand-alone novella that can be read and enjoyed separately.

AUTHOR'S NOTE

I love India and I've wanted to set a story there for a long time. Of course, it's impossible to do justice to such an incredible culture in one action adventure story, but I hope that you enjoyed the attempt. I always enjoy hearing from readers who have looked into the research behind the book, so here are some of the aspects that went into it.

The initial idea came from a statue of Shiva Nataraja that I saw in the Museum of Delhi back in 2006 when I visited the Taj Mahal and Varanasi, which also features in *Stone of Fire*, ARKANE book 1. Then I read about the huge statue at CERN, Himmler's fascination with Hinduism, and the phrase spoken by Oppenheimer, and the conspiracy was born.

You can find the pictures behind the book here on Pinterest: www.pinterest.com/jfpenn/destroyer-of-worlds

India

I tried to make the Indian locations as close to reality as possible, although I haven't visited all the sites in person. I did visit the synagogue in Fort Kochi on a cycle trip through South-West India and many of the other places have a flavor from my own travels, supplemented by other research from books and documentaries. Here are some of them:

The Story of India by Michael Wood. Book and documentary series.

Sacred India documentary.

Ganges documentary.

West Meets East. Kumbh Mela documentary with Dominic West

In the Land of Shiva. Book by James O'Hara

The real tomb of Shah Jahan and his wife Mumtaz are beneath the main room of the Taj Mahal, and there are conspiracy theories of a Shiva temple below. The Aghori truly are a pretty scary sect, and the worship of Kali does range from mainstream temples to reported child sacrifice in rural areas, although of course, I have used extreme examples for an exciting novel!

Rwanda

In earlier books, I hinted at Marietti and Jake's experience in Africa and as I thought about the idea for *Destroyer of Worlds*, it seemed to me that Marietti would have wanted to stop the same thing happening again. I was nineteen in 1994 when the genocide happened and I remember seeing pictures of the mass graves. Researching the atrocity was difficult, but part of the reason that I write is to challenge my own thinking. If you want to read more, I recommend *We Wish to Inform You That Tomorrow We Will be Killed With Our Families: Stories from Rwanda* by Philip Gourevitch.

MORE BOOKS BY J.F.PENN

Thanks for joining Morgan, Jake and the
ARKANE team. The adventures continue …

Stone of Fire #1
Crypt of Bone #2
Ark of Blood #3
One Day in Budapest #4
Day of the Vikings #5
Gates of Hell #6
One Day in New York #7
Destroyer of Worlds #8
End of Days #9
Valley of Dry Bones #10

If you like **crime thrillers with an edge of the supernatural**,
join Detective Jamie Brooke and museum researcher Blake
Daniel, in the London Crime Thriller trilogy:

Desecration #1
Delirium #2
Deviance #3

If you enjoy **dark fantasy,** check out:

Map of Shadows, Mapwalkers #1
Risen Gods
American Demon Hunters: Sacrifice

A Thousand Fiendish Angels:
Short stories based on Dante's Inferno

The Dark Queen

More books coming soon.

You can sign up to be notified of new releases, giveaways
and pre-release specials - plus, get a free book!

WWW.JFPENN.COM/FREE

ABOUT J.F.PENN

J.F.Penn is the Award-nominated, New York Times and USA Today bestselling author of the ARKANE supernatural thrillers, London Crime Thrillers, and the Mapwalker dark fantasy series, as well as other standalone stories.

Her books weave together ancient artifacts, relics of power, international locations and adventure with an edge of the supernatural. Joanna lives in Bath, England and enjoys a nice G&T.

* * *

You can sign up for a free thriller,
Day of the Vikings, and updates from behind the scenes,
research, and giveaways at:

WWW.JFPENN.COM/FREE

* * *

Connect at:
www.JFPenn.com
joanna@JFPenn.com
www.Facebook.com/JFPennAuthor
www.Instagram.com/JFPennAuthor
www.Twitter.com/JFPennWriter

For writers:

Joanna's site, www.TheCreativePenn.com, helps people write, publish and market their books through articles, audio, video and online courses.

She writes non-fiction for authors under Joanna Penn and has an award-nominated podcast for writers, The Creative Penn Podcast.

ACKNOWLEDGMENTS

Thanks to my editor, Jen Blood, for her help with the book, and my proofreader, Wendy Janes. Thanks to Jane Dixon-Smith for the cover and interior print design.

Thanks to Uma Aiyer for her beta reading and helpful comments about Mumbai. A huge thanks to the Pennfriends, who support my book launches, and thanks to all my readers, for enabling me to tell the stories that burn in my heart.